Kill By Night

ILLUSTRATIONS *by* **Gavontae Bailey**

About the Author

GaVontae Bailey began writing his first book at the age of 16 but stopped after losing interest and not fully seeing his vision. During this break, he focused on coding and developing new skills. Two years later, the passion for writing returned, this time with a mind full of ideas and inspiration. As a fan of horror, action, and science fiction movies, this inspiration would lead to the creation of several gripping titles, including *Kill by Night 2*, *Red Rain*, *School Detention*, and *It Comes Alive at Midnight*. And also Science fiction books such as *The War of Time* in development. His commitment to the craft reflects his deep appreciation for thrilling and imaginative storytelling.

Introduction

By Ga'Vontae Bailey

The beginning of new adventures, but for eight friends, it becomes the start of a nightmare they never expected. Seeking to celebrate their last days together in a remote cabin deep in the woods, they are excited for a week filled with fun, laughter, and unforgettable memories. But beneath the surface, something sinister lurks. As old secrets begin to resurface and shadows from their past come to life, the friends quickly realize they are not alone. Their peaceful escape turns into a deadly game of survival when a relentless killer, hell-bent on revenge, begins to hunt them down one by one and the nightmares don't end there. Instead, Draven follows them and hunts down and finds the rest of them its 12 more to go.

Contents

About the Author ii

Introduction iii

Chapter 1 A Night to Remember 1

Chapter 2 Blood in the Shadows 12

Chapter 3 Trail of Blood 24

Chapter 4 Blood and Betrayal 35

Chapter 5 The Mask's Return 46

Chapter 6 The Silent Countdown 58

Chapter 7 The Beginning of the End 70

Chapter 8 Blood and Horror 81

Chapter 9 Blood on the Deck 92

Chapter 10 Blood and Ashes 103

Chapter 11 Draven last stand 112

Chapter 1
A Night to Remember

Eight friends went on a trip for their graduation party: DayDay, Geo, Steve, Mark, Sarah, Faith, Maya, and Zuri. They arrived at a private house in the woods. "What is this?" Maya exclaimed. "We're staying here for the party, so everyone shut up and get out of the car," Mark replied. They got out of the car, and got their bags from the trunk, and brought them inside the house. "Wow, this looks nice," DayDay said, impressed. "Yeah, we're spending a week here," Mark settled. "Faith and I are going to the store to get some food for the house," Steve announced. Steve and Faith head to the nearby store to stock up on food and supplies for the week. "We need to make sure we have enough to eat," Steve said as he grabbed the car keys. Faith nodded in agreement. They quickly looked in the kitchen to make a list of things that they needed.

"I'll drive," Faith offered, wanting to make the most driving use of their time. Because she had just got her license, they both slipped on their jackets and headed out the door, the cool breeze of the woods greeting them as they made their way to the car. The drive to the store was relatively short, but it allowed Steve and Faith to take pictures in the serene beauty of the surrounding forest. The road wound through tall, ancient trees whose leaves rustled gently in the wind.

The sunlight filtered through the canopy, casting dappled shadows on the ground. "It's so peaceful out here," Faith remarked, her eyes wandering over the landscape. Steve agreed, his mind momentarily drifting 132away from the task at hand. They chatted casually about their excitement for the trip, their plans for the week, and their hopes for the future now that they had graduated.

Arriving at the small local grocery store, Steve and Faith quickly grabbed a cart and began moving through the aisles with purpose. They picked out a variety of items, ensuring there was something for everyone.

Fresh fruits and vegetables, snacks, drinks, and ingredients for meals filled their cart. "We should get some marshmallows for a campfire," Steve suggested with a grin, and Faith eagerly added them to the pile. They also selected a few local delicacies, wanting to try something new during their stay. With the cart full, they headed to the checkout, chatting with the friendly cashier about their plans for the week. Bags in the trunk, Steve and Faith drove home. Their hearts were light, eager for a week of fun, laughter, and new memories.

Meanwhile, everyone else was taking their bags up to their rooms. "Who wants some weed?" Geo asked. "Yes!" everyone responded in unison. Geo went upstairs to grab two bags of weed, and Mark turned on the music. Six hours later, Steve and Faith returned from the store. Zuri and the others went outside to help bring in the grocery bags. A man watched them from a distance, but when Mark looked, he saw nothing. Steve locked the car door, and everyone went back inside to continue the party.

The next day, everyone was hungover. DayDay got up and started cooking breakfast. When it was ready, he called everyone downstairs to eat. While they were eating, DayDay stepped outside, with his phone already in his hand, and dialed Terrell's number. The evening air filled his lungs as he paced back and forth on the porch, waiting for Terrell to pick up. The phone rang a few times before Terrell answered. "Hey, Terrell, it's DayDay," he began, his voice filled with excitement. "I need you to do me a favor. Can you invite everyone from school to a party tonight? It's going to be epic!" Terrell said you got it and it's a good time, agreed without hesitation. With a grin on his face, DayDay ended the call and went back inside, eager to start setting up for the night. Meanwhile, Terrell got to work.

He scrolled through his contacts and sent group

messages to all his friends and classmates. He knew the perfect spots to catch everyone: group chats, social media, and even a few direct calls to make sure the word spread fast. "Hey everyone, DayDay's throwing a huge party tonight! You don't want to miss it. Be there!" Terrell's messages buzzed through phones and lit up screens. They excited their schoolmates. The responses came in quickly. Friends confirmed they would attend and bring snacks, drinks, and music to make the night unforgettable.

Later that day, seven cars and trucks pulled up. Geo looked out the window. "Who are those people?" Geo asked. "I invited them. Terrell did it," DayDay said. "What the hell? I thought it was just us," Steve replied, annoyed. DayDay opened the door, and people started streaming in. "Before we start partying, there's only one rule: do not break anything. Now, let's party!" Mark announced. Zuri put on some music. While everyone was partying, Malik and Aaliyah went outside to walk around.

Twenty minutes later, Terrell asked Maya, "Have you seen Malik and Aaliyah?" "They went outside. Stop worrying and join me upstairs," Maya said. "You're right. Let's go," Terrell agreed. Meanwhile, Malik and Aaliyah were talking about moving in together.

Suddenly, Draven, the killer, appeared and chopped Malik's head off with an axe. Aaliyah screamed and tried to run back to the house, but Draven dropped the axe, picked up his bow and arrow, and aimed at Aaliyah. As she ran and cried, Draven released the arrow, striking her in the heart. Her body dropped to the ground.

Later that night, everyone inside was high and oblivious to the horror unfolding outside. As the party raged on, Geo began to recount a chilling story from their past. "Remember that time in middle school when those kids died?" Geo started, his voice trembling slightly. "Well, what if I told you we are those kids who were with the kids that died?" The room fell silent, everyone staring at Geo in shock. "Geo, shut the hell up! That was supposed to be a secret!" Steve hissed, clearly angry and scared. Zuri looked around, trying to lighten the mood. "Who's rolling up?" she asked. "Me, pass it here," Sarah replied, trying to ignore the rising tension.

Downstairs, the group continued to get more messed up, oblivious to the danger lurking outside. Draven was methodically poking holes in everyone's tires, ensuring there would be no easy escape. The music thumped loudly, masking the sinister sounds of metal piercing rubber. As the night grew darker, the air inside the house grew thick with smoke and tension. No one noticed the shadowy figure moving around the perimeter, preparing for the next phase of his plan. The friends continued to party, unaware that their fun would soon become a nightmare they'd never forget.

In an attempt to shake off the unsettling feeling, Geo continued the story. "No, we aren't the ones who died. That was Vontae and Jazmyne. Remember? We went inside old man Draven's house and started exploring. Vontae and Jazmyne went downstairs while the rest of us were upstairs talking." He paused, the memory clearly haunting him. "Geo, this is not the time," Steve interrupted, but Geo persisted. "I found a lighter and flicked it on, tossing it by the curtain. I didn't mean for it to catch fire." The room grew tense as their past mischief set in. Their laughter faded to an uneasy silence as they realized the possible consequences.

Meanwhile, Draven sabotaged the outside, trapping his prey. As the night wore on, the friends inside remained unaware of the danger. They were lost in their intoxication and the loud, pulsing music. The shadow of their past and the looming threat of Draven converged, setting the stage for a night that would forever change their lives.

Later that night, when everyone was asleep, Draven slipped inside the house. His eyes gleamed with malice as he surveyed the sleeping figures in the rooms. The soft sounds of their breathing filled the air, a stark contrast to the ominous stillness that now enveloped the house. With cold determination, Draven crept from room to room. His hands were steady as he brandished his weapon: a gleaming blade that glinted in the moonlight. He approached his victims, one by one.

His heart filled with a twisted satisfaction as he watched fear flicker across their sleeping faces. Draven struck with brutal efficiency. His blade sliced the air, deadly and precise. He unleashed his fury on his unsuspecting friends. Blood sprayed across the walls, mingling with the soft light of the moon as Draven's rampage continued unabated. The air was thick with the stench of death as Draven moved from one room to the next, his savage onslaught leaving a trail of destruction.

Next morning DayDay came downstairs, trying to cook, but he saw a bloodbath. He ran upstairs to wake up his friends and said, "Let's go! Everybody is dead downstairs." Faith said, "Really? It can't be. Let's go pack our bags." Steve said, "It's your fault, DayDay!

You told that story." DayDay replied, "It's not my fault. I just told a story, but let's get out of here. Let's stop arguing. But we cannot go through the front door." Geo asked, "Why?" DayDay said, "We don't know if the killer is still out there."

Steve said, "I'll go check." Steve went downstairs to see if it was clear. He stepped over bodies until he reached the door. He opened the door slowly, looked both ways, and then called out to the others, "It's clear downstairs, but step over the bodies." Out of nowhere, Terrell jumped and scared Steve. Terrell said, "Are you OK? What happened?" He pushed the door open and saw bodies on the floor. He said, "What is this? Y'all killing people now?" Steve responded, "No, you idiot.

DayDay woke up and saw bodies on the floor. He came and got us. We are going to leave."

Terrell said, "We can't go anywhere. I tried to leave; all the tires are flat. I slept in my car. Somebody came outside at night who was bloody. He had a mask on, but I was high. I didn't know what I saw. I think I saw that; I'm not sure, but someone has been here." Steve asked, "What color was the mask?" Terrell said, "It was a black mask with a crack in it. It looked like the mask was on fire." Mark said, "It couldn't be." Sarah asked, "Is Vontae trying to kill us?" "That's impossible; he died in the fire with his sister Jazmyne," Geo responded. "They never had a funeral. They never found the bodies." "If we can't go anywhere, let's go find some weapons and kill this son of a bitch," Zuri said, determined. As they armed themselves with whatever they could find, the friends huddled together, forming a tight circle. The realization hit them hard there was no way out.

The house, once a place of joy and celebration, had become a prison. With every creak of the floorboards and every whisper of the wind, their fear grew. They knew they were being hunted, and the day was far from over. Their only hope was to survive until the next morning, to outwit a killer driven by a relentless need for revenge. "Where are Malik and Aaliyah?" Terrell asked, worried evident in his voice."

They're not back yet," Maya replied. "They are probably dead," Steve said grimly. "Where did they go?" Maya wondered aloud. "I saw them leave, and I guess they never came back." "They're dead. They probably were the first people to die," DayDay concluded with a grim nod. "No, I don't believe it. Malik is my cousin. I can't leave him out there. He is still alive, and I'm going to save him," Terrell declared, leaving the house to search for Malik and Aaliyah. "He's going to die. You never leave the house by yourself if the killer is outside waiting for you," Mark warned. "Terrell is acting white." "Wait, Terrell! I am going with you," Maya screamed, running after him.

Five hours later, as the sun was setting, Mark became anxious. "Where are Maya and Terrell? They should've been back by now."

"Who has their phone?" Steve asked. "Our phones are about to die, and we don't have any service," DayDay, Zuri, Sarah, and Geo responded in unison. "I have two bars," Faith said, handing her phone to Mark.

"We should look for them before nightfall," Steve suggested. "Why should we look for them? If they die, they die. I am not going to die trying to save somebody's life," Geo retorted. "They are our friends," Steve insisted. "I can make some more friends," Geo said coldly. "Who are you calling?" DayDay asked Mark. "The police," Mark replied. "Did they pick up?" DayDay questioned.

"Yeah, they said they are going to send someone out here, so we just gotta wait it out," Mark said.

Later that day, Terrell and Maya moved cautiously through the dense trees, their breaths visible in the cold night air. The eerie silence of the woods was broken only by the crunch of leaves beneath their feet. Every shadow seemed to hold a threat, every rustle a warning. Back inside, the remaining friends fortified their positions. Their nerves frayed as they realized their dire situation. Geo held a baseball bat tightly, while Zuri armed herself with a kitchen knife.

"We need to stick together," Sarah urged, her voice shaking. "If we scatter, we're done for." They nodded in agreement. "Where are the police? It's been three hours, and it's already night," DayDay said. "

They should've been here. Call again," Steve suggested.

Meanwhile, Terrell and Maya continued their desperate search. They found the gruesome remains of Malik and Aaliyah. Their lifeless bodies filled them with horror and sadness. Maya fell to her knees, sobbing uncontrollably. Terrell, fighting back his own tears, pulled her to her feet. "We have to go back," he whispered urgently. "We need to warn the others." But, as they turned to leave, Draven emerged from the shadows. His bloodied axe gleamed in the moonlight.

Terrell pushed Maya behind him and stabbed Draven with his pocket knife. Draven just looked at him and pushed him to the ground. Draven raised his axe and chopped off Terrell's arm.

Chapter 2
Blood in the Shadows

This gave Maya enough time to run back to the house. Draven looked at Maya as she ran, then turned back to Terrell and chopped off his head. Maya ran back to the house, screaming for help. "Y'all hear that?" Steve asked. "That's Maya!" DayDay exclaimed, rushing outside to save her. Maya sobbed, "He killed him. He really killed him."

DayDay made it to Maya, picked her up, and carried her back to the house, locking the door behind them. "What the hell happened? Where is Terrell?" Mark demanded. "Vontae killed him. He chopped off his arm and his head," Maya said through her tears. "Don't call him Vontae. Vontae died with his sister," Zuri said. "We should just call him Draven because he died in the Draven house when old man Draven was a killer. He killed his whole family," Geo suggested. "You're right.

We shouldn't call him Vontae because Vontae is our friend's name. We didn't mean to leave them in the house; we didn't even know they were inside until the next day," Zuri added. "We should've gone back to see.

But where is Draven now?" Steve said, pacing back and forth. "He's probably outside watching us. It's time for us to leave. He's just one person; let's take him out together," Mark replied. Out of nowhere, something dropped from the chimney. DayDay looked up in horror. "Who in the hell is that?" he exclaimed.

Suddenly, Draven, covered in blood and with a crazed look in his eyes, emerged from the shadows. Draven moved with terrifying speed, his blade glinting in the dim light as he lunged at DayDay. DayDay tried to dodge, but Draven was too fast. He grabbed DayDay by the throat, lifting him off the ground effortlessly.

DayDay struggled, kicking and punching, but Draven's grip was unyielding. With a swift motion, Draven plunged his blade into DayDay's chest. The sound of flesh tearing and bone cracking echoed through the room.

DayDay's eyes widened in shock and pain. Blood poured from the wound, staining his clothes and pooling on the floor.

"Go!" Geo shouted. Everyone ran for the door as Draven pulled the blade out with a sickening squelch. He let DayDay's lifeless body drop to the ground. "What was that?" Steve asked, panicking. "I think that was the killer," Geo said, trembling. "We can't beat him; we need the cops," Sarah said, her voice shaking. Mark suddenly remembered. "I have guns in my car. They should be in the trunk under the floor."

Zuri responded angrily, "All this time you had guns in your car? We should've gotten those earlier!" "Oh, my bad. I was high. I wasn't thinking we were gonna die," Mark admitted sheepishly. "Both of you shut up. Let's go back to the car and get the guns to kill him," Steve ordered. They slowly made their way to the car. Mark unlocked the trunk, and they grabbed the guns. "Where is Draven? It's so quiet out here," Zuri whispered.

She went back inside the house to see DayDay's body. As Sarah watched from the door, it suddenly slammed shut. Zuri looked to her left, and there stood Draven, his axe ready. The last thing she saw was the blade coming down. The others outside heard her scream, echoing their own rising terror. Mark rushed inside the house and started shooting. But Draven wasn't there and Zuri's body was missing. Mark told everybody that was outside to come in. Let's go and kill him. Steve checked the back while the others checked everywhere else. Meanwhile, Draven was at his cabin. He tied up Zuri to the electric chair and connected wires from it to the C-4 before he left. He grabbed the gag and put it in her mouth. Then, he left and rigged the door. If someone opened it, the cabin would blow up.

Meanwhile, Geo heard the police sirens. Maya ran outside, screaming for help. The officer said, "Put down the gun." Maya dropped her gun. Mark and the others came outside. When the officer saw their guns, he shouted, "Put down the guns, now!" Geo said Hell Naw it's a killer out here trying to kill us. Steve asked, "What is your name, officer?" The officer replied, "Officer Castle." Mark said, "You took too long to get here.

People died." Officer Castle asked, "Where?" "In the house," said Faith. Officer Castle rushed inside.

Meanwhile, Maya and Sarah went into his car to call for backup. When Officer Castle came back and saw them in his car, he said, "Get the hell out!" Mark said, "Don't talk to them like that." Steve, Sarah told them to hurry before this officer killed them.

Officer Castle got his radio to call for backup. Mark said, "What do we do now? I'm not waiting to be killed." "Fact," said Geo. "Brother," added Steve. "Did y'all hear that?" Officer Castle said, "Get in the house now!" Everyone ran to the house. The officer searched everywhere. But, when he looked up, Draven dropped down from the roof. He used his axe to chop off Officer Castle's arm. Geo drew his gun and shot Draven twice.

Draven fell. Steve dragged Officer Castle inside the house while Geo checked if Draven was dead. Geo tried to take off Draven's mask. When he lifted it,

Draven grabbed Geo's leg, took his blade, and sliced his ankles. Geo collapsed on the ground and started to scream. Maya ran outside to pick up Geo. As Draven got up, he aimed his bow at Geo's neck. He released the arrow. It went through Maya's arm and into Geo's neck. Mark started to shoot everywhere. Faith tried to help Maya, but it was too late. Draven aimed at Maya's head and fired. Blood splattered everywhere. Steve picks up Faith and closes the door. Mark said he can't die. Geo shot him two times and he got back up and killed him. Officer Castle said we have to wait until my back up gets here. Mark said I'm not waiting on no cop to get here. Mark grabbed his gun and shot Officer Castle in the head. Sarah said what did you do? You just shot an officer. You go to jail. Mark replied, "I'm not going to jail. We're gonna die anyway. We're not leaving here."

He's trapped us. He poked holes in our tires. We can't drive out. You're right," Steve said. "We can't escape." "We can only escape if we kill Draven," Faith said. "How do we kill Draven?" Geo shot him twice. Draven got up and killed Geo and Maya. Steve said I will go out there to kill him. Stay here Sarah locks the door behind Steve. Steve braced himself as he stepped outside. He was determined to find Draven and end this nightmare.

Inside, the friends huddled together. The weight of

their situation pressed on them. Tension hung in the air.

Steve moved cautiously through the dark, his eyes searching for any sign of the killer. Meanwhile, the police backup arrived, sirens blaring and lights flashing.

The officers quickly spread out to search the area. This gave the terrified friends inside a brief sense of security. One officer, Officer Daniels, approached Mark and the others. He asked for any information they could provide.

"There's a cabin nearby," Faith said, her voice shaking. "Draven might be hiding there." "Show us the way," Officer Daniels commanded, gathering a small team to accompany Faith. In the dense forest, Faith's heart pounded with fear and resolve. They reached the cabin and immediately noticed the eerie stillness surrounding it. The officers moved in, their weapons drawn and ready. They cautiously approached the door, aware that it could be rigged with traps. Inside the cabin, Zuri struggled against her binds. Her eyes widened as she saw the officers approaching through a small window.

She tried to scream, but the gag muffled her cries. One officer carefully opened the door. The moment it swung open, explosions rocked the cabin. The officers were thrown back, and flames engulfed the structure.

Faith is injured trying to run back to the house. The friends heard the explosions and saw the firelight flickering through the trees. Panic set in as they realized their situation was growing direr by the minute. Steve, hearing the explosions, quickened his pace. He was desperate to find Draven before anyone else got hurt.

As Steve neared the burning cabin, he spotted Draven in the shadows. His eyes gleamed with a twisted satisfaction. Steve raised his gun, aiming at Draven.

But he dropped his gun and said let's fight man to man. Draven agreed and dropped his axe. They clashed in a violent struggle, each using all their strength. Steve managed to land a few blows, but Draven's strength was overpowering. Just as it seemed Draven had the hand, a gunshot rang out, echoing through the night.

Draven staggered back, a look of shock and rage on his face. Steve looked up. Officer Daniels, who had survived the explosion, stood a few feet away, his gun still smoking. The explosion sent debris flying in all directions. For a moment, it seemed no one could have survived the blast. Ten officers had perished that night, their sacrifice weighing heavily on the survivors. But, a large, sturdy table had shielded

Officer Daniels. It had absorbed most of the explosion. The table had been knocked over by the force, but it had provided enough cover to save his life. As the dust settled, Daniels quickly assessed his situation. He had only minor injuries. The blast had left him with a ringing in his ears and a few cuts and bruises, but his training and instincts kicked in. He crawled out from under the table, his mind focused on the mission at hand.

With adrenaline coursing through him, Officer Daniels grabbed his gun. He was determined to finish what they had started. He moved through the debris, his eyes scanning for any sign of Draven. The chaos of the explosion had disoriented him, but his resolve remained unshaken. "It's over," Officer Daniels repeated, his voice firm.

Draven fell to the ground, his body finally succumbing to the injuries. Steve and Officer Daniels stood over him. The nightmare was finally over. Relief was palpable. As they were walking back to the house, they saw Faith on the ground, barely breathing. So Officer Daniels picked up and carried her to the house. Sarah opens the door and Mark says Draven is dead! Steve applied to say yes. We killed him. Officer Daniels shot him. Officer Daniels said, "Shut up and help me save your friend." Meanwhile, Draven began to stir. His eyes opened. They gleamed with a cruel, evil light. Despite the bullet wound and the blood-soaked clothes, he pushed on. He grabbed his axe and bow, then walked back to the house. As Sarah went upstairs to get some sleep. She heard something. So she got up to check and saw the window was open.

She screamed in fear as Mark rushed upstairs. "What happened?" he asked. "It's blood by the window," Sarah said, her voice shaking. "Draven is dead. More cops are on the way." Sarah cried in Mark's arms.

Officer Daniels said we are going to be ok Draven is dead Faith said are you sure? Because one of our friends shot him and he got up and killed him. Officer Daniels said, "I'm sure." What happened to Officer Castle? Before Steve could answer, Sarah and Mark came back downstairs. Sarah couldn't shake the uneasy feeling that something was wrong.

As Mark held her, she tried to steady her breathing.

Downstairs, the rest of the group huddled together, the tension thick in the air. Suddenly, a loud crash echoed through the house. Everyone froze, their eyes wide with fear. Steve whispered, "What was that?" Officer Daniels motioned for everyone to stay quiet as he moved toward the source of the noise, his gun drawn. In the dim light, Officer Daniels carefully navigated through the house. He found the living room window shattered, glass scattered across the floor. His heart pounded in his chest as he approached the window, peering out into the darkness.

Just as he turned to signal it was safe, Draven swung his axe and chopped off Officer Daniels' head. Steve then told everyone to go upstairs. Everybody went upstairs. When Steve looked, Draven was gone. He looked everywhere downstairs. Mark said so Draven is not dead. He just killed the last officer. What do we do now Sarah said "We got to kill him and chop off his head?"

Faith said shut up. Do you hear that? Out of nowhere, Draven shot Sarah twice in the heart and once in the head. Mark saw him and fought for his bow and arrow until they both fell downstairs. Faith screamed. Draven got up, grabbed his bow, and shot Mark in the heart. Steve picked up Draven's blade and stabbed him repeatedly. Draven fell down. "Is he dead?" Faith asked. "Yeah," Steve replied. Faith picked up Steve and they walked out of the house, sitting on the porch together. Five minutes later.

Draven got up and walked to the back. He grabbed a bag, then walked to the living room. He changed Mark's outfit to someone else's. Then, he put a fake mask on Mark and left through the back door. Meanwhile, Steve stood up and walked back inside.

Faith asked, "What are you doing?" Steve replied and said to chop off Draven head Steve picked up his ex and chopped off his head. Faith said I heard a police silence. When the police arrived, the scene was one of horror and confusion. They asked what happened Steve replied and said a murderer killed all of my friends. Office Jackson said Damn it's a bloodbath in there I almost threw up. Meanwhile Draven is walking down the street until a CIA agent stops him. Draven looks at the CIA name tag and it says Agent Zay. Zay said get in here Draven got in the car. Meanwhile Steve called Isaiah and said we need you to work this case Isaiah said what case? Steve said the case that I'm part of. Do you remember Vontae Isaiah said yea I do he was my best friend and his sister was my girlfriend.

Steve said Vontae is not dead. He killed our friends. We won't call him Vontae. His new name is Draven because he survived the old Draven house. What? I'm on the way," Isaiah said. "Is he coming?" Faith asked. Steve said yea, Meanwhile CIA Zay said "are you ok let's go to the hospital" Draven nod. CSI Isaiah called Captain Hill about the case. Captain Hill replied yes, you can. We didn't think the killer was dead. I think him switched clothes. Isaiah said, what?

Thank you for the info. I'll call you when I have something. Steve and Faith were going home.

Tomorrow, they would examine "Draven's body" to determine whether Vontae was truly Draven. Isaiah calls his cousin an FBI agent. Agent Jerry Robins asked Isaiah about his son, Malik. His head was chopped off. Jerry broke down in tears. He asked if the killer was dead. Isaiah said no. They blamed it on Vontae, aka Draven. Jerry said, "Vontae?

That name sounds like the old case. Vontae and his sister, Jazmyne, died in a fire." Isaiah said that's not true.

Chapter 3
Trail of Blood

When I started to work for the CSI, I looked into the case. They never found the bodies, so they just said that two kids died. Agent Jerry said that was Vontae and Jazmyne. I said, "Yeah, so I'm going to find Draven, the killer." Agent Jerry hung up and packed his bag to go to Redwood City, California. The next morning, Steve and Faith went to the mortuary to see "Draven's body." A doctor pulled back the sheet to reveal the body. Faith collapsed in despair and started screaming. Steve said that was not Draven, but Mark.

Isaiah appeared and said, "It'll be okay. I'm on the case. You need to go to a safe house." Steve picked up Faith and left with the police to give them a description of Draven. Now, all the police knew what he looked like.

Meanwhile, Draven was patched up and ready to kill again. Zay took Draven to the police station, dropped him off, and drove away. Captain Hill saw Draven with C4's. So, he told his office to arrest him. It was a tense standoff as ten officers tried to arrest Draven, a man wielding a fearsome axe. Despite their training and numbers, they were no match for him. Draven is killing everyone. Captain, call the S.W.A.T. and say, "code black, office down."

Captain Hill dropped the phone and looked at all his officers on the ground dead. Captain Hill walked outside and said Draven drop your axe and fight me now! Draven drops his axe and walks to Captain Hill while Draven is walking to Captain Hill. Captain Hill was shooting at Draven but missed. Draven picked up Captain Hill, threw him to the ground, and squeezed his eyes shut. Then, he stepped on his head. Captain Hill's brains were everywhere.

After that, Draven left the manslaughter outside. He walked inside and planted C4 around the police station. Then, he went to a tall building to see the police station. Five minutes later, four S.W.A.T. trucks pulled up. They saw the horror Draven caused. Forty men jumped out of the trucks and ran inside the precinct to check for survivors. The phone rang, and one of the men answered it. The precinct blew up and killed 40 men. Draven walked out the building and broke inside a car and stole it.

Meanwhile, Agent Jerry just arrived in California. He heard that 51 police officers are dead. Isaiah pulled up at the airport to pick him up.

Agent Jerry Isaiah is telling Jerry everything. 51 cops didn't die. At least 60 officers died. I got a team to recover everything after the police department got blown up. Jerry said stop the car. I think I know what he was looking for. Isaiah started to drive again and said just talk Jerry Damn. Jerry said "Draven isn't just acting out of rage," he said, his voice filled with concern. "There must be a reason behind his actions." His thoughts raced as he considered the possible motives behind the violence. Isaiah got a call from his team and they said two files were missing.

Isaiah's team said DeShawn and Darnell Harris's files are missing. Jerry said he knew the names. They used to be friends with a group of kids, and I think Steve and his friends were in it. Isaiah stopped the car and told his team to find everyone who was friends with that group. I think Vontae, aka Draven, was in it. If that's the case, he's not done hunting them. Jerry said he thought he knew how many people were in the group! Isaiah said TELL ME! Jerry said twenty. Isaiah said Draven killed six from that group. Jerry said, what if they left him and his sister in the house when it was on fire? Isaiah said eighteen left the house. Draven killed six in that group.

So, we are looking for ten people. We got Steve and Faith. Jerry's fingers trembled slightly as he dialed the number for the FBI. The situation had escalated beyond what he and Isaiah could handle alone. They needed serious backup. The phone rang twice before an authoritative voice answered. "This is Director Thompson."

"Director, this is Agent Jerry Robins. I'm in California

on a case that's spiraling out of control. I need immediate support." Jerry's voice was urgent, laced with the gravity of the situation. "Calm down, Robins. What's going on?" Director Thompson's voice was steady, but the concern was evident.

Jerry took a deep breath. Then, he explained the events that led to the massacre at the police station. He detailed the link between Draven and a group. They had abandoned him and his sister in a fire years ago. "Director, we've identified that there are ten more potential targets on Draven's list. He's already killed six, and he's not going to stop until he's finished his mission. We need to get to these people before he does," Jerry concluded.

There was a brief pause on the other end of the line. "This is a high-priority situation, Agent Robins. We'll mobilize a task force immediately. I'll also notify local law enforcement in San Francisco, Las Vegas, and Los Angeles. We'll coordinate efforts to locate and protect the remaining targets. Stay on the line. I'm patching up our field offices in those cities now." Jerry exhaled in relief, though the tension in his chest remained. He could hear Director Thompson relaying the details to other agents. His voice was calm but commanding. The severity of the situation was not lost on anyone.

Isaiah glanced at Jerry as he finished the call. "What's the plan?" Jerry said the FBI will mobilize a task force.

They'll coordinate with local law enforcement to find the remaining targets. They think someone is working with Draven. Isaiah said we are here. Meanwhile, Steve called DeShawn. He said to watch his back. Draven is coming to kill us. DeShawn hung up and left the bar to get his gun. He grabbed it and checked the magazine to make sure it was loaded.

Then, he tucked it into the waistband of his pants and pulled his shirt over it. He couldn't afford to look weak, not when his life was on the line. He called everyone to meet him at the old Draven house. One by one, they agreed, their voices a mix of fear and determination. They knew the risks, but they also knew that hiding would only delay the inevitable. Draven was coming, and they had to be ready.

Five minutes later DeShawn pulled up at the house

The place had long been abandoned, a relic of the past. It still bore the scars of the fire. One by one, the others arrived. Marcus, Jessica, and Tyrone looked wary. They glanced around, expecting Draven to leap from the shadows at any moment. They gathered in a tight circle in front of the house, the weight of what they were about to face pressing down on them. The betrayal that had left him scarred and vengeful. They had been a group once, a tight-knit gang of friends. But that fire had changed everything. Now, they were being hunted by the boy they had abandoned. Draven locked all the doors and waited for them. DeShawn got a text from Steve. Before he could read it, Draven came out of nowhere and chopped off DeShawn's hand. Marcus was shooting, but Draven was too fast. He didn't hit him. Draven got close to Marcus and squeezed his face. Jessica started to scream. Tyrone ran to the door, but it was locked. Draven threw his axe at Tyrone.

Tyrone was bleeding out. The axe hit his heart. Jessica was crawling on the floor. Draven stepped on her head twice. DeShawn looked in horror and said, "We never had a chance." As he struggled to his feet, his vision blurred. He saw Draven standing over Marcus's lifeless body, his chest heaving from the fight. There was no mercy in Draven's eye, only a cold, remorseless determination. DeShawn broke the door and left.

Draven got his axe, walked close to DeShawn's hand, and picked up the phone. He saw Steve and Faith's location.

Later that night Jerry reviewed the files on the remaining group members. Three of them were still unaccounted for in this city. The FBI had sent agents to their last known addresses. But, Jerry knew better than to trust old info. Draven had shown that he was always one step ahead, and that made him deadly. Out of nowhere Agent Zay said "Is there anything that i can do?"

Isaiah said "Who is you?"

Agent Zay said I work for the CIA. They told me to come down here to help with the investigation. Isaiah frowned, clearly on edge. "We've got this under control," he replied, curt. But, his voice hinted at uncertainty. Agent Zay didn't back down. "With all due respect, you need all the help you can get.

This guy isn't just some random killer. He's smart, strategic, and relentless. If we're going to stop him, we need to work together." Jerry, sensing the urgency in Zay's voice, stepped in. "Isaiah, he's right. Draven is a different kind of threat. We need all the resources we can get."

Isaiah hesitated for a moment, then nodded. "Alright, Zay. You're in. But remember, we're calling the shots here." Zay gave a brief nod, understanding the gravity of the situation. "Understood. What's our next move?" Jerry leaned over the files, his mind racing. "We need to find the remaining targets before Draven does. He's working off an old list, but we don't know how accurate his information is. "We need to cross-reference everything. Check for any recent changes in addresses, phone numbers, or anything that might give us a lead."

Isaiah added, "And we need to do it fast. Draven's

already killed six people from that group. If we don't move quickly, there'll be more bodies."

Out of nowhere, a phone rang. It was Jerry's.

Someone said they heard gunshots at old man Draven's house. Jerry dropped the phone and told everyone to run. Draven had killed again. Everyone got ready, but Isaiah and Zay said, "We can check on Steve and Faith." Jerry said, "Okay, but be safe." Meanwhile, DeShawn was walking, trying to find help. Little did he know, Draven was right behind him with his axe. DeShawn's bleeding stump showed, and his face twisted in pain. He had no idea where he was going; his only thought was to find help, to survive.

The night was filled with an unsettling silence. Only his labored breathing and the faint rustling of leaves in the wind broke the silence.

He approached a small house on the edge of town. A light was on inside. So, DeShawn dragged himself to the front door. His vision was blurred from blood loss and exhaustion. He raised his good hand to knock. The door creaked open. A woman stood in the doorway, shocked at DeShawn's bloodied, battered form. "What happened?" she gasped, her eyes wide with concern.

DeShawn's voice was barely a whisper, his strength fading fast. "Who...who are you? I need your help."

The woman stepped forward, catching him as he collapsed. "I'm Tasha," she said quickly, trying to keep him conscious. "You're safe now, just hold on." DeShawn's vision darkened. He heard Tasha's frantic voice calling for help before he lost consciousness. The world around him faded to black as his body gave in to the overwhelming exhaustion and pain. As DeShawn lay unconscious, Draven pursued him. His axe glinted in the moonlight. The night was far from over, and he had more work to do. His mind was a storm of vengeance, driving him forward as he followed the trail of destruction he had set in motion.

Five minutes later DeShawn woke up and said where I am?

Tasha replied and said you are in my house covered in blood.

What happened? Because I am not with that. What did you bring inside my house? Deshawn said to slow down. I was on my bike and fell off. I hit the glass door.

Next thing you know, my hand was off. I was walking, trying to find help. I'm knocked on every door, but they didn't answer but you did thank you. Tasha said don't thank me yet. I'm calling the police. DeShawn waited, don't do that because I already did. They were taking too long to come so I started to walk. Out of nowhere, they heard something loud up upstairs. Deshawn said what that was with fear in his voice. Tasha said I could check Tasha walk upstairs to check all of the rooms. Nothing was in the rooms so she made her way back downstairs. DeShawn said everything is clear. Tasha was about to answer, but her voice caught. Before she could speak, Draven plunged his blade into her back.

The force of the attack lifted her off her feet as she convulsed, her body twitching violently. Deshawn, stunned and horrified, muttered, "Oh hell naw, "he tried to get up, but he slipped in a puddle of blood. Draven drops Tasha lifeless body and picked up DeShawn and took him to the kitchen Draven put him on the counter and opened the drawer. He picked up a knife and stabbed him with it. He picked up another knife and slid his throat. Draven looked over DeShawn's lifeless body.

His breathing was steady, and his mind was focused.

This was just the beginning.

There were more names on his list, more people who needed to pay. He wiped the blood from his axe and turned away, disappearing into the night like a phantom. Police were coming down the street to check on old man Draven's house when I got there. It was a bloodbath. "Not again!" Jerry said. "He's killing people non-stop. We need to stop him now. How many did he kill?" The officer said 81 and counting Jerry said y'all see that it's a blood trail. Jerry followed the trail and stumbled on a house with an open door. He ran inside. It was a massacre. Blood covered the walls and floor. He called his boss and asked to bring everybody. We need everybody in this case. This is getting out of hand Draven is killing everybody who comes in contact with the group. He doesn't need to go to jail, he needs to die. The officer beside him nodded solemnly, the gravity of the situation clear in his eyes. "What do we do, Jerry? How do we stop him?"

Chapter 4
Blood and Betrayal

Jerry took a deep breath, his mind racing. "We can't wait for him to strike again. We need to be proactive.

We know who he's targeting, so we need to get to those people first. We protect them, or we use them as bait. Either way, we end this." He pulled out his phone and dialed Isaiah. "Isaiah, its Jerry. Listen, Draven's not just going after the group he's killing anyone who comes near them. We have to take him down. I'm done playing defense." Isaiah's voice was grim on the other end. "I hear you, Jerry. We've got leads on the remaining targets. Zay and I are heading out now to secure them. But Jerry... if it comes down to it, are you ready to do what needs to be done?" Jerry's grip tightened on the phone. "I've never been more ready, Isaiah. This ends tonight. Draven's left us no choice."

Isaiah paused, then replied, "Alright. We'll make it here. But Jerry... be careful. Draven's not the same kid before the fire. He's something else now, something dangerous." Jerry ended the call and looked around at the officers preparing for the next move. "Listen up!" he barked, drawing their attention. "We're going after Draven. No more waiting, no more reacting. We take the fight to him. And when we find him, we don't hesitate. We will end this." The officers exchanged grim looks, then nodded in agreement. They knew what they were up against a man who had lost his humanity, consumed by vengeance. They couldn't afford to show mercy. As the team geared up, Jerry felt a cold determination settle over him. Draven had crossed a line, and there was no going back. The hunt was on, and this time, it was going to end in blood. "Let's move out," Jerry ordered, leading the charge. The night was far from over, and with every passing moment, Draven was getting closer to his next target. But Jerry was done being a step behind. He was going to find Draven, and he was going to make sure this nightmare ended once and for all. At Steve and Faith's location, Isaiah and Zay arrived. Steve said, "Have you found the others?" Zay replied, "We are looking for them now."

Steve then said, "I forgot to tell you. One of our friends was close to Draven and his sister. They were cousins. His name is Lamar Brown." Isaiah said, "Damn! Tell us everything. All their names. If you hold back, you'll go to jail for putting lives in danger."

Steve told them about everyone tied to Draven: Lamar Brown, DeAndre "DayDay" Davidson, and Geovanni "Geo" Jackson. Me too. Mark Johnson, Sarah Anderson, Faith Mitchell, Maya Lewis, Zuri Robinson, and the Harris twins, DeShawn and Darnell.

Lastly, Raven Walker, Imani Davis, Jada Williams, and Naomi and Nia Brooks, and Darius and Isaiah Davis. You were just a little older than us. But, you were in a group. You wanted to go in the house. Isaiah said that was a long time ago. I regretted it because now Draven is trying to kill us. Isaiah called Jerry and told him every name that Steve gave him. Isaiah's hand tightened on his phone as he ended the call with Jerry.

Steve looked up, his expression a mixture of fear and determination. "Isaiah, if Draven's targeting all of us, there's one more thing you need to know. After the fire, Lamar Draven's cousin went off the grid. None of us have heard from him since. Isaiah nodded. "We'll find Lamar before Draven does. I'll get Jerry's team on it.

But you need to help us, Steve. I need you to think. Are there any places Lamar would go? Anywhere he'd feel safe?"

Steve rubbed his temples, trying to recall any details. "Lamar used to talk about a cabin his family had up near the mountains. He said it was his dad's before he passed. That might be where he is." Isaiah glanced at Zay, who nodded and began making a call, likely to set up a team to search the cabin. They were finally getting somewhere. Isaiah turned his attention back to Steve. "And the others? Did they have any other places they'd run to if things got bad?" Steve hesitated, glancing at Faith before answering.

"I don't know. We lost touch over the years."

Isaiah made a mental note of the information. They had leads, but Draven was still out there, hunting them down one by one. He needed to stay a step ahead. Faith finally spoke, her voice shaky. "Isaiah, what if we don't find them in time? Draven... he's not going to stop." Draven made it to the safe house and he put sleeping gas inside the vent. Isaiah walked over to her, placing a reassuring hand on her shoulder. "We will find them, Faith. And we'll stop Draven. I promise. But you need to trust us and stay safe."

Zay hung up his phone and joined them, his face serious. "I've got a team heading to the cabin and another checking out the factory. We've also put out a BOLO for Lamar. If he's still around, we'll find him."

Isaiah nodded. "Good. Jerry's coordinating with local law enforcement, so we've got the city covered.

Draven's not going to slip through this time. We're closing in." The tension in the room was thick, but there was a sense of purpose now. They had a plan, and every second counted. Isaiah could feel the weight of his past decisions bearing down on him. He had been part of that group. He had seen the fire and its aftermath. Now, those choices were haunting them all.

But this time, he was determined to make things right.

Isaiah's phone buzzed, a text from Jerry: FOUND MORE BODIES AT OLD MAN DRAVEN'S HOUSE. DRAVEN'S ESCALATING. BE ON GUARD.

Isaiah clenched his jaw, his resolve hardening. "Alright, everyone. We're moving. Because Draven is coming here searching for the rest of the locations. Draven's on the move, and we need to be faster." Faith was looking and said, "I don't feel so good." Steve caught her as she hit the ground. Isaiah's heart skipped a beat at the sight of her collapse. Steve barely managed to catch her before she hit the floor, his face a mask of panic.

Isaiah rushed over, kneeling beside Faith, checking her pulse. It was there, but weak. She was breathing, but her breaths were shallow, labored.

"Faith, hey, stay with us!" Isaiah called out, but she didn't respond. Her eyelids fluttered, her skin turning pale. Steve looked at Isaiah, fear evident in his eyes. "What's happening to her? She was fine just a minute ago!" Zay was already moving, checking the room's surroundings. His eyes scanned the vents and the windows, searching for anything unusual. "Something's not right," he muttered. "This isn't just panic, something's affecting her."

Isaiah stood up, his mind racing. He turned to Steve, who was still holding onto Faith. "Steve, take her to the bathroom, get some fresh air on her face. We need to keep her conscious." Steve nodded, struggling to lift Faith. Isaiah helped, and together they got her into the small bathroom, laying her on the floor near the sink.

Steve splashed water on her face, his hands shaking. Zay's voice came from the other room, tense. "Isaiah, get over here!" Isaiah left Steve and Faith and rushed back into the living room. Zay was standing near one of the vents, his expression grim. "There's a smell. You notice that?" He pointed towards the ceiling vent. Isaiah

Sniffed the air and caught a faint, sweet odor. It was subtle but unmistakable. Isaiah's eyes widened. "Sleeping gas. Draven must've found us. He's trying to knock us out." Zay nodded, his jaw clenching.

"We need to get out of here now. If he's using gas, he's planning to take us all out." Isaiah moved quickly, pulling his shirt over his nose and mouth. He shouted to Steve, "We need to move! Now! Get Faith up; we're leaving!" Steve, struggling with Faith, called back, "She's not waking up! I don't think she can walk!" Isaiah swore under his breath. They were running out of time. "Zay, help me with the windows. We need to air this place out, fast." They rushed to open the windows, letting the cool night air rush in, diluting the gas. But it was clear that it wouldn't be enough; the gas had already started to affect them. Isaiah felt a slight dizziness, and he knew it was only a matter of time before they'd be too weak to escape.

Suddenly, there was a noise outside, a soft thud against the door. Isaiah's blood ran cold. Draven was here. Zay caught Isaiah's eye, his expression tense. "We're not going to get out of this without a fight." Isaiah nodded, adrenaline pushing back the dizziness. "Get ready. We won't let him take us down without a fight." Zay moved to the door, peering through the peephole. He could see a dark figure moving outside, a shadow passing across the lawn. Draven was stalking them, waiting for the gas to take full effect. Isaiah grabbed his gun from his waistband, the weight of it reassuring in his hand. He glanced at Zay. "We do this smartly. We won't let him get the drop on us." Zay nodded, pulling his own weapon. "On your signal."

Isaiah moved towards the door, taking a deep breath. He looked back at Steve, who was still trying to rouse Faith. "Steve, stay down. Protect her. We're going to end this." Steve's eyes were wide with fear, but he nodded, pulling Faith closer. Isaiah turned back to the door, his heart pounding. He could feel the effects of the gas, his mind starting to blur, but he forced himself to stay focused. This was their only chance.

Isaiah nodded to Zay, then opened the door. He stepped into the night, his gun raised, ready for the fight. The cool air hit him, clearing his head just enough. He could see Draven's silhouette in the darkness, his axe glinting in the faint light.

Isaiah slowly grabbed his phone from his pocket and dialed Jerry as he waited on Jerry to pick up. Zay said what are you doing? We can't last inside this house. Finally, Jerry picked up and Isaiah said he is here.

Bring everybody here now Jerry told everybody the location. Everyone grabbed the stuff and went to the spot. Isaiah dropped his phone. It stumped on it and told Draven this is tonight. Zay screamed at Isaiah, "Steve has collapsed!" Isaiah shot Draven five times. He missed two and three connected Draven felt the bullets but he still walked towards Isaiah. Isaiah was not scared. He was ready to face Draven. Draven swung his axe.

Isaiah blocked it, then grabbed Draven's axe and threw it on the ground.

Isaiah stood tall, adrenaline pumping through his veins. "Fight me!" he shouted. Draven, silent and menacing, raised his hands, ready for battle. Isaiah lunged forward with a punch, but Draven sidestepped with ease, moving like a shadow. Draven swung back, landing a hard punch to Isaiah's gut. Isaiah grunted in pain. He quickly retaliated, throwing a wild punch. It grazed Draven's cheek.

Draven's face twisted in anger as he charged at Isaiah, throwing rapid punches. Isaiah dodged as many as he could but took a hit to the jaw, stumbling back. He managed to grab a nearby branch and swung it at Draven, hitting him on the shoulder. Draven grunted, momentarily stunned, but quickly regained his footing.

He kicked Isaiah's legs out from under him, sending him crashing to the ground. Draven moved to pin him down, but Isaiah grabbed a handful of dirt and threw it into Draven's eyes. Blinded, Draven stumbled back, wiping his eyes. Isaiah took the chance to get up, grabbing the branch again. He swung it at Draven's head, but Draven caught it mid-air, snapping it in half with his bare hands. The two men faced each other, breathing heavily. Isaiah threw a desperate punch, but Draven caught his fist, twisting his arm painfully. Isaiah cried out in pain but managed to kick Draven in the nuts, breaking free.

With one final push, Isaiah tackled Draven to the ground, pinning him down. Draven struggled, but Isaiah managed to keep him down just long enough for Zay to run up with handcuffs. They quickly restrained Draven, finally bringing the fight to an end. Isaiah stood over Draven, breathing hard. "It's over," he said, feeling a mixture of relief and exhaustion. Zay picks up the axe and swings it at Isaiah's legs. Isaiah collapsed on the ground bleeding out. Say why are you doing this? Zay said because he is my son I raised him after the fire. It was terrible after what happened. So, I burned two fake bodies. I took out Vontae and Jazmyne, but his sister was dead. He wasn't, so I took him to a hospital, and he survived. His mask was on his face. The fire almost burned through his mask, but it didn't. He can't talk, and something told him to kill everyone in the way. So, he's going after the FBI. He was angry after what happened. He wanted to kill them myself, so I helped him. I trained him how to fight and how to kill and I helped him find everybody who was in that group. When I found out you were part of that group, I had to kill you. I just learned you wanted to go inside the house.

In my head, I'm thinking, "Why are you working for CSI? You're a murderer." Isaiah was spitting out blood. He said it was my mistake, but I didn't deserve to die like this. Zay took off the handcuffs and picked up Draven. He gave Draven back his axe. Zay called Lamar and said to hurry up. Lamar replied, "I'm already here." I'm inside the house. Lamar walked outside and said, "I'm ready." Draven gave his mask to Lamar. Zay said, "He gave you his mask because he has to heal.

Chapter 5
The Mask's Return

"He wants you to kill people. He will be back to take his mask. Oh yeah I almost forgot Where is the body?"

Lamar said in the car. Zay and Lamar got a body from the car and put it next to Isaiah's body. Lamar said everybody will think Draven is dead. Zay said that's the plan and don't start killing immediately. Wait two months later then kill and I need you to stab me in my stomach. Lamar said I got you and he stabbed Zay.

After that Lamar and Draven started to leave, Zay went to the porch and laid out two minutes later. You can hear police coming to save the day. Jerry and his team and two ambulances arrived Jerry saw Isaiah first and said WE NEED HELP! Three paramedics came to check if Isaiah was alive. One said, "He's barely breathing. We need to take him now." Jerry replied, "Don't let him die. He's a friend." Jerry saw Draven's body and said, "We need to burn it. But first, go in the house." His team rushed to the first porch and saw Zay, bleeding out.

One of Jerry's agents, Kai, said, "Jerry, you need to see this. It's Zay." Kai checked his radio and said, "He is alive." Jerry asked two paramedics to help him out.

Kai moved into the house, searching for any other victims.

He found Steve and Faith unconscious but alive, lying on the floor. He called back to Jerry, "Steve and Faith are inside! They're out cold, but they're alive." Jerry waved over two paramedics. "Get them to the hospital, too." Jerry looks at "Draven's body" and pulls out his gun, shoots Draven in the head five times and burns his body. Three weeks later, Steve and Faith moved in together. They are trying to move on with their lives.

Zay just got out of the hospital. Isaiah is in a coma. Jerry got a promotion to assistant special agent in charge.

Two months later Lamar sat in his car, the streets illuminated by the flickering lights of the city. The mask of Draven lay on the passenger seat beside him, a constant reminder of his purpose. His mission was to spread fear, to make sure everyone knew that Draven was still out there, and no one was safe. He was driving but stopped at a motel. He had been planning something big, to instill fear in everyone. But his goal wasn't to go after the group directly, it was to kill their family and friends. Lamar had a different plan for the group.

He was going to gather them all in one place and let

Draven kill them off. When he stopped the car he found his first victim at the motel. He put on the Draven mask, feeling its weight settle over his face.

The mask was more than a disguise. It was a symbol, a legacy of terror that had started with Draven and would continue with him. As Lamar stepped out of the car, he glanced around, the mask obscuring his face. He reached the backseats of the car, pulling out a large duffel bag. It was heavy, with two axes, one bow and arrow, a grenade, and a torch, as he approached the man outside, smoking a cigarette. The man said. Who are you? Without a word, Lamar swung one of the axes in a wide way, the blade gleaming in the dim light. The man barely had time to react before the axe connected, cutting clean through his neck. His head fell to the ground, and his cigarette dropped. Then, a dull thud followed as his body collapsed. Blood pooled around the body, staining the concrete.

Lamar stood over the lifeless body for a moment, breathing heavily behind the mask. He felt no remorse, no hesitation. This was just the beginning. The mask, the blood, the violence it was all part of the plan. He must ensure everyone knew Draven's wrath was alive, still hunting, and that there was no escape. He turned back to his car, wiping the axe blade clean before putting it back into the duffel bag.

And get his bow and arrow and the other axe. He walked up to the door of one of the motel rooms, where a flickering light could be seen through the curtains. Lamar heard muffled voices inside. A man named Rick and a woman named Kate were arguing about bills. Rick didn't have the rent because he lost everything gambling. Now, he lives in a motel. Lamar banged on the door, the sound echoing through the empty parking lot. The voices inside went silent. I heard hesitant footsteps at the door. "Who is it?" Rick called out from the other side. Lamar didn't respond. He just stood there, breathing slowly, the mask concealing his identity.

The door cracked open, the chain still latched. Lamar shot through the crack and hit him in the shoulder. Then. Lamar kicked the door open with a powerful thrust of his leg. The chain snapped, and the door flew inward, slamming against the wall. Kate screams and tries to run away. Lamar grabbed her by her neck and tossed her outside. She was unconscious. Rick said "What are you doing?" Lamar picked up. Rick and choke slapped him through the dresser that the TV was on.

Lamar aimed at. Rick shot him, then shot him twice in the heart. Lamar went to his car for gasoline. While spreading it around the hotel, Kate woke up and went to the front door. Lamar saw her and dropped the gasoline. He chased after her.

Kate made it inside and called for help. Lamar caught her, squeezed her head, and her blood splattered. After that, he doused the rest in gasoline and set it on fire.

But the night was far from over. As he drove away from the motel, leaving the scene behind, he knew it wouldn't be long before news of the murder spread. And when the time is right, he will bring everyone together, just as he had planned. Meanwhile, Steve is having a nightmare about the night. He tossed and turned in bed, sweat beading on his forehead, his face in agony. In his dream, he was back on that fateful night when he saw his friends die. Faith tried to wake up Steve and said it was just a dream to get up Steve shouted, jolting awake.

He was breathing hard, his heart racing. Steve looked around, trying to shake off the remnants of his nightmare. His chest heaved as he took deep breaths, trying to calm himself. "It felt so real, Faith. I could hear them. Faith nodded sympathetically, rubbing his back in slow circles. "I know, Steve. But it was just a dream. Draven's gone. He's dead. Jerry burned his body, he told us and they got his mask.

Steve ran a hand through his hair, still shaken. "Yeah, I know. But it's like... I can't get it out of my head.

Every time I close my eyes, he's there, waiting." Faith squeezed his hand gently. "You're safe now, Steve.

We're both safe. We just need to stay focused and keep moving forward. We'll get through this."

Steve nodded, though the fear still lingered in his eyes. "I hope you're right," he muttered, lying back down. As Faith lay down beside him, Steve stared at the ceiling, his mind replaying the nightmare over and over. He couldn't shake the feeling that Draven wasn't really gone, that somehow, the terror was far from over.

Meanwhile, Jerry got a call from the police. They said to check the bodies. One was headless, one had three arrows in it, and the last had no face. "I'm on my way," Jerry, the assistant director, said. Meanwhile, Darnell, Raven, and Imani were in a car. They were driving to California. Darnell had just found out his brother had died. He needed to get away and clear his head. Raven and Imani were there for support, hoping a change of scenery would help him cope. "I still can't believe he's gone," Darnell said quietly, gripping the steering wheel.

Raven reached over and squeezed his shoulder, offering silent comfort. Imani stared out the window, her mind elsewhere. They had all lost people, but Darnell's pain was fresh, raw.

A few miles behind them, another car headed in the same direction. Jada, Naomi, Nia, and Darius were crammed inside, excitement buzzing in the air. They had all received a call a few days ago telling them they'd won a free vacation. A luxury cruise in California, all expenses paid. They first thought it was a scam.

But, everything checked out. Now, they were on their way to an amazing getaway. "I still can't believe we won!" Naomi exclaimed from the backseat, a huge grin on her face.

"I know, right?" Jada replied, glancing at her in the rearview mirror. "It's just what we need. Some time to relax and get away from everything like college and bills and homework." Darius, sitting in the passenger seat, nodded in agreement. "Yeah, this is gonna be great. Just us, on the cruise, and no worries." As they drove, none of them had any idea that they were heading straight into Lamar's trap. Lamar's plan was coming together perfectly. The group had no reason to suspect anything. They thought they were going on a vacation, but Lamar had other plans. He would gather them all in one place, and when the time was right, Draven would come.

The pieces were falling into place, and soon, the nightmare would begin again. Faith woke up Steve and surprised him with a vacation Steve said vacation?

Faith said a cruise I got the tickets a few weeks ago. I hope you're not mad. Steve said I'm not mad when we go, Faith said. Today at 3 o'clock Steve said OK I will be ready as he walked downstairs. To go cook. Faith made some coffee. Meanwhile, Jerry arrived at the crime scene. And said what do we have here in a burn building? Kai said three bodies and we'll think we might know who did it Jerry said who? Kai said it was Draven. The killer left an axe. Jerry said it can't be. We burned his body, right? Isaiah killed him. Kai said, "What if he didn't? What if he stopped killing for a while?" Jerry's face fell. He called the hospital where Isaiah was. Jerry ran to his car. Kai asked, "Where are you going?" Jerry shouted over his shoulder, "I'm going to see Isaiah to protect him. If Draven's back, someone needs to watch him.

He is still in a coma" Kai watched as Jerry sped off meanwhile, Faith and Steve were packing up the last of their bags.

The excitement of the upcoming cruise had wiped away the nightmare. Faith turned on the TV and the news.

She saw the burnt building. Three bodies had been pulled from the wreckage, but they were not identified. Steve got up, turned off the TV, and said, "No more dead bodies. We are going on vacation." "My bad. I was just checking the news," Faith said. "Are you ready?" "Steve nodded.

"Yeah, I'm a bit nervous about leaving everything behind." Then she came downstairs, smiling brightly.

In Darnell's car, Imani, still staring out the window, turned her head slightly to look at Darnell. "Grief is like that," she said. "It doesn't make sense. But we'll get through this together." Darnell said it was my fault I shouldn't have let him go to California by himself.

Raven said no it's not as they arrive at the morgue.

Darnell, Imani, Raven walked in and the doctor said are you Mr. Darnell? Darnell said yes. The doctor said to come this way. At the door, Darnell broke down crying.

Imani picked him up and said to be brave. Darnell stood up and walked to DeShaw's dead body. "Who killed him?" he asked. The doctor said a person named Draven. But a hero named Isaiah killed him. Isaiah is in a coma with no legs.

Everyone in that room looked at each other and said it couldn't be. They asked the doctor who else Draven killed. The doctor said, "I can't tell you that. But, I can give you three tickets to a cruise. I was going to take my family, but we're not going anymore."

Darnell said, "A cruise? My brother is dead! I'm not going to have fun. I have to plan his funeral." Raven said, "You can let your parents do that. If you go on the cruise, it will take your mind off things." Imani grabbed the tickets and said, "Thank you."

Raven stepped forward, placing a hand on Darnell's arm. "Darnell, we're not saying this to ignore what happened. We're saying it because we care about you. We know you're hurting, we hurting too. DaShaw was a friend but we need something to cool our mind Darnell said y'all are right let go. Meanwhile, Jada, Naomi, Nia, and Darius talked excitedly about the cruise. The thought of sun-soaked decks, exotic drinks, and the freedom of the open sea had them all in high spirits.

The four friends had been through a lot recently, and this surprise vacation felt like a blessing.

"Do you think they'll have those big pools like on TV?" Nia asked, leaning forward from the back seat, her eyes shining. "Absolutely," Darius replied, grinning. "We're gonna eat like kings and queens. Naomi said "I read online that the cruise has a 24/7 snack bar, alcohol bar and at least five different restaurants." Ten minutes later, they did it to the boat. Jada said it was a huge cruise ship they went on. Darius spotted a crewmate in a crisp uniform and approached him. "Hey, man, when do we set sail?" The crewmate, a middle-aged man with a friendly smile, glanced at his watch. "We depart at six o'clock sharp," Darius read his name tag and said thank you Tom. Meanwhile, Jerry arrived at the hospital to see Isaiah. But Zay was already in his room. Jerry asked, "How did you get in here?" Zay replied, "I saw on the news that three bodies were found in the building. So, I rushed to the hospital to check on Isaiah." Jerry said, "Oh, ok. My team thinks Draven is back." We found his weapon he always uses at the scene: a damn axe and three arrows. If he's alive, Isaiah could be in danger, and not just him. Everyone who's ever crossed paths with Draven could be a target."

Zay glanced at Isaiah, who lay unconscious in the bed, hooked up to various machines. His face was pale, and his body looked frail. "If Draven is back, then we need to act fast. We can't let him get to Isaiah or anyone else." Jerry nodded. "I've already got my team locking down the cruise terminal. We think Draven's planning something there. But I can't help shake the feeling that this is all part of some bigger plan." Zay mind racing and said. "The cruise is a perfect place to trap a lot of people in one location. If Draven's involved, there's no telling what he might do."

Jerry pulled out his phone, dialing Kai's number. "We need to increase security. Get more eyes on that cruise ship. Kai said we don't even know what he looks like.

We never saw Draven's face. Jerry said to look for someone hiding their face. Kai said we will be ready to take him down." Zay watched as Jerry made the call and he stepped out of the room and made a call to Lamar. Lamar answered the phone. "What do you want?" Zay whispered, "Be careful. Everybody is looking for Draven. Where are you?" Lamar said, "I just finished sending a package to their families. Then, I'm going to the cruise." Zay pacing the hall telling him to be safe and said "Draven we're going on a cruise later. When are the bombs? Lamar said at six o'clock sharp. Zay said, well, that's when the cruise leaves."

Chapter 6
The Silent Countdown

Lamar hung up and got ready. But, first, he had to go to the hospital to kill Jerry. Zay went back and told Jerry, "I have to go. I think we got a lead." Jerry said, "Go." Zay left. Little do you know he was going to die tonight? Back on the cruise ship, Darnell, Raven, and Imani finally made it aboard. They looked around and saw Nia. Raven ran to Jade and said, "I miss you." Jade's eyes widened. "It's been years since I saw y'all." Darius walked up to Darnell. "I'm sorry for your loss. He was a close friend. Do you know who killed him?" Imani stepped up and said, "Draven." Naomi said, "I remember that name. Isn't that the house we were in years ago? It caught on fire and Vontae and Jazmyne died."

Raven said, "Yeah." I miss them. I miss all of us. There were twenty of us back then, and now there are eighteen. I wonder how Zuri and the rest are doing. Darius said, "Did Isaiah become a CIA agent?" "Yeah," Darnell said. "The doctor told us that he killed Draven. Now, he's in the hospital in a coma." "Damn," Jade said. "He was the oldest. He wanted to go inside the old man Draven's house." Out of nowhere, Faith came running over, tears streaming down her face. She threw her arms around Darnell from behind, hugging him tightly. "I'm so sorry for your loss," she sobbed.

Raven said y'all here too. Everybody was happy until Naomi asked where Mark or Geo was. Steve answered and said "They... They didn't make it. Draven got them. Vontae is Draven. We called him that because he's not the same Vontae we once knew." Naomi said "really so he survived the fire?" Faith said, "Yea, I saw the mask." Darnell was shocked. It says, "Stop talking about it.

We're on a cruise. Let's just have fun." Lamar made it to the hospital and went to Isaiah's room. He stepped inside, and Jerry said, "Who is that?"

"I'm Lamar," he replied. "I know who you are. You're Draven's cousin." Lamar said, "Guilty as charged." Jerry grabbed his gun, but Lamar was already close and stabbed him. Jerry fell down. Lamar wiped the blade on Jerry's shirt, then walked out. He took the elevator down and left through the doors to get to his car. Lamar checked the time on his phone. He had just enough time to make it to the cruise before it set sail and made his way to the cruise. Draven's plan was coming together, and Lamar would make sure it succeeded. As he sped down the highway, a twisted smile spread across his face. The nightmare was far from over. It was just beginning. Kai was calling Jerry but he didn't pick up. He called four more times and

Jerry still didn't pick up. Kai called his team member and said we need to go to the hospital now.

Something's wrong. Jerry's not answering his phone, and he was supposed to be with Isaiah. I'm on my way.

Meet me there as soon as you can." "Got it," his teammate replied, urgency in his voice. Kai hung up and grabbed his keys, rushing out of his office. As he got into his car and started the engine, a feeling nagged at him. Things were spiraling out of control. It seemed impossible that Draven was alive. Yet, too many things pointed to it. At the old, abandoned warehouse, Zay stood before Draven, who was sitting in the shadows and said let go. Draven got up and walked to the pen and paper writer down "is their family still alive and we need to go."

Zay picked up the paper. "Not for long. They'll be dead in ten minutes." Lamar just made it onto the cruise with his large duffel bag.

When he got on, Jade saw him. She jumped into his arms. "Where did you go?" Lamar said, "I just had to clear my mind. My cousins died." Jade screamed to the others, "Lamar is back!" They rushed to him and said welcome back. Where were you? Lamar said just clearing my head. Meanwhile the doctors came in and saw Jerry on the ground bleeding out.

One of the doctors screamed *HELP! HELP!*

Nurses and medical staff scrambled, bringing in a stretcher and medical equipment. They worked quickly. They moved Jerry onto a stretcher and wheeled him out of the room to the emergency surgery unit. Kai just made it to the hospital and rushed upstairs to Isaiah's room. He saw blood on the floor and he asked a doctor what happened, whose blood is that the doctor said it's an agent named Jerry. Kai said, "Where is he?" The doctor said in the emergency room. He was attacked. He's in surgery right now." Jerry's team made it to the hospital. They were asking questions saying where is our captain? Is he okay? Kai said he was attacked in Isaiah's room. We think it was Draven. This confirms our worst fear: Draven is alive, and he's here." The team fell silent, the weight of Kai's words sinking in.

The agent, who had spoken, clenched his fists. "How is this possible? We need to find him. He won't stop until he's taken everyone down."

Kai nodded. "I know. We need to secure the hospital and make sure Isaiah is protected. If Draven's willing to attack here, he's not going to stop. But right now, our main priority is Jerry. We need to make sure he pulls through." The doctor pointed down the hall. "They've taken him to the OR. It was bad, really bad. They're doing everything they can." Kai and the team nodded, trying to steady their thoughts. They needed to keep a clear head. On the cruise ship, Lamar stood with his old friends. They talked about how fun this trip would be and told stories of their past adventures. He listened to their stories and nodded at their memories. But, he hid his true thoughts. He could feel Jade's eyes on him, searching for the Lamar she once knew. He had to use all his self-control to hide his feelings. As the group chatted, the ship's horn blared again, signaling its departure from the dock. Lamar checked his phone, his heart racing as he scanned the delivery confirmations.

One by one, notifications popped up on the screen. Each marked the successful arrival of a package. His lips curled into a satisfied smirk. Meanwhile, miles from the cruise ship, Naomi's and Darnell's parents' houses creaked open. The parents stepped onto their porches. They said, "I got a package from my daughter," and, "I got a package from my son." As the mothers bent to pick up the packages, they walked inside to open them.

In an instant, everything changed. The packages exploded, a deafening roar shattering the evening calm. Fire and smoke billowed out, the force of the blast ripping through the air.

Windows shattered. Debris flew in every direction. The shockwave echoed down the quiet suburban streets.

Neighbors ran out of their houses, eyes wide with horror as they took in the sight. Flames licked at the remains of the houses, charred wood and smoke filling the sky. The once-peaceful neighborhood was thrown into chaos. People screamed, some in fear, others shouting for help. A Friend neighbor grabbed her phone, hands trembling as she dialed 911. Her voice was a mixture of panic and disbelief as she spoke. "There was an explosion next door! I think someone's dead! Please, send help!" In the distance, sirens of police cars and fire trucks approached. They grew louder with each passing second. Red and blue lights flashed against the night. They illuminated the horror that had unfolded. Then the rest of their Parents got blown up. Lamar checked his phone again and it said all of the Packages had been opened.

Lamar went to the restroom. He put a phone jammer in the wall so nobody could make or receive calls. He was trying to reach the engine room. Jade said where is Lamar? Darnell said he got up to use the restroom i think.

Looked up, her brow furrowed.

"I tried to call my mom, but I couldn't get through. It just went straight to voicemail. It's weird. We should have a signal out here." Faith shrugged casually,

"Maybe we're just in a bad spot for reception. You know how these big ships are tons of steel, signal interference. I'm sure it's nothing."

Steve chimed in, agreeing. "Yeah, Jade, don't worry about it. We're here to relax, right? Your mom's probably fine." Jade nodded, but a flicker of unease remained in her eyes. She forced a smile, pushing the worry to the back of her mind. "Yeah, you're probably right."

As Lamar reached the engine room, he carefully set the final charges. His hands moved with the precision of someone who had done this many times before. Each bomb was placed strategically, hidden from sight but powerful enough to do the job. He set the timers, each one synced with the others, all set to detonate at the exact same moment. Lamar straightened, taking a step back to admire his work. The countdown had begun, and there was no stopping it now. In just a few hours, everything would change. He turned and walked back up the stairs, merging into the flow of passengers. The night was falling, the sky darkening over the open sea.

Music played softly over the ship's speakers, and the sound of laughter filled the air. Lamar felt a thrill run through him, a sense of power and control. Lamar returned to the room. He said, "Let's go to the bar." Everyone agreed and they headed to the bar.

Meanwhile, back at the hospital, Jerry is out of surgery. His team was inside his room two minutes later. Jerry woke up and said, "Where is Lamar?" Kai said we don't know why? Jerry said because he was the one who stabbed me. Kai called agents that were available to track down Lamar. He is dangerous shot to kill. So it wasn't Draven that blew up the motel, it was Lamar.

Jerry said I think so but I think Draven is still alive. And I think Zay is helping Draven and Lamar because when Zay left. Lamar came in and stabbed me. Kai said we are looking for an agent named Zay to kill him on site.

He is dangerous. Put his face all over the news. And it said if you see this man go get help don't face him he will kill you. Kai felt the vibration of his phone against his leg. He pulled it out, reading the news alerts that had begun to spread. Reports of the explosions were already hitting the media. Kai said we have 11 bomb sightings. Jerry replied, "I have to go. People are dying." Kai said, "No. You just had surgery. You can't go. We'll take care of it." Kai called the captain and he didn't answer. As Kai tried to call again, a thought struck him. What if Draven or his accomplices had cut their communications? If the cruise ship was indeed Draven's target, everyone aboard was in danger, and they had no way of knowing.

Meanwhile, Zay saw the news. He said, "We need to do plan B." Draven nodded. Zay took them to the insane asylum. When they arrived, Zay killed all the guards. Draven opened the front door. All the crazy people were right there. Zay stepped in and said, "Who wants to kill? If you do, step up. Get an outfit and a mask. Your mask will look like Draven's. Your outfit will look like his too. We don't want the FBI or the police going to the cruise ship. So, we need everyone to grab a mask and an axe and kill anyone you want." Chaos was the new normal. The situation was spiraling out of control. Kai's thoughts raced as he processed Jerry's revelation. If Lamar and Zay were with Draven, the danger was greater than they had thought. They were running out of time on the cruise ship. There had been eleven bomb sightings and a communication blackout.

Back in the hospital, Jerry tried to push himself up, grimacing in pain. "You don't understand, Kai. This isn't just about revenge. They're planning something huge, something deadly. Draven... he's not just some madman; he's methodical, ruthless, smart. He's got a plan, and I don't think we've seen the worst of it yet." Kai shook his head, trying to maintain control over the situation. "Jerry, you need to stay here and recover.

You've done your part. Now let us handle this." But

even as he spoke, Kai felt the weight of the task ahead pressing down on him. If Draven, Lamar, and Zay had been planning this for years, they were already steps ahead. And now with Zay's face on the news, every moment counted.

Meanwhile, at the insane asylum, Zay stood amidst the chaos he'd unleashed. The asylum, a place once meant to contain madness, had become a breeding ground for it. The guards lay dead, and the inmates unhinged, violent, and now armed looked to Zay as if he were a twisted messiah. Draven's influence had seeped into their minds, and Zay, his loyal lieutenant, was there to guide them. Draven watched from the shadows, a small smile playing on his lips as Zay addressed the crowd.

"You've been locked up, caged like animals. But tonight, you're free. Tonight, you get to be who you were meant to be predators. And those FBI and Officers? They're your prey. Now, take your weapons, take your masks, and make them fear the name Draven." The asylum erupted in cheers, a symphony of madness, as the inmates rushed to arm themselves. They put on the masks and outfits. They became a horde of Draven's faceless soldiers. Zay handed out axes, knives, and anything else that could be used to inflict terror. It was no longer just a plan; it was a nightmare given life.

As the newly armed and masked inmates prepared to leave, Draven left. Zay stopped him and said be safe you are going to cruise Draven nod and walk out the door and get into the car and drive out.

Zay led the first wave of inmates to the waiting buses. They were to be taken to the city. As they boarded, Zay turned back to the buses, filled with masked, armed inmates. His pride swelled. He had spent years in the shadows, working quietly, but tonight would be his moment. He would be the one to bring Draven's vision to life, to unleash a wave of terror that would be remembered forever.

After a final glance at the now-silent asylum, Zay signaled for the buses to depart. The guards had been massacred. The engines roared to life, and one by one, the vehicles pulled out, heading toward the city. Zay took a seat at the front of the lead bus, his eyes fixed on the road ahead. The city lights twinkled in the distance, unaware of the storm that was about to descend upon them. As the convoy made its way toward the city, Zay couldn't shake the excitement bubbling within him. Every detail had been meticulously planned, every variable accounted for.

The police and FBI were focused on the cruise ship, leaving the city vulnerable. By the time they realized what was happening, it would be too late. As the city skyline grew closer, Zay's mind shifted back to the task at hand. The inmates, now fully armed and eager for blood, were ready to spread terror through the streets.

Chapter 7
The Beginning of the End

They would strike at the city's heart, causing chaos. This would divert attention from their true target, a cruise ship.

Zay could picture the headlines: "Draven and the Massacre in the City."

The thought twisted a smile on his face. This was what they had been building toward for years. The climax of their efforts, their pain, their rage. And now, it was all coming to a finish. As the buses approached the city, Zay stood up, turning to address the inmates. "Remember," he said, his voice like a general's. "Go break into a house and kill them in their sleep. Be quiet. Don't make a noise as you kill them. We're doing this for the cops and the FBI. Tonight, we will show them we are unstoppable." No mercy, no hesitation. You know your targets.

"Spread out, cause as much destruction as you can. This is only the beginning."

The inmates cheered, their voices a mix of madness and prediction. Zay nodded, satisfied. He signaled for the buses to split up. Each would head to a different part of the city. The plan was simple: hit multiple locations at once. This would overwhelm the city's defenses. Then, retreat before the authorities could respond.

As the buses dispersed, Zay's bus continued toward the city center. He had his own role to play, and it was the most crucial part of Draven's plan. While the others created chaos on the streets, he would be the one to deliver the final blow. Zay's phone buzzed in his pocket, and he pulled it out to see a message from Draven: is everything set. Zay replied with a single word: Always. He slipped the phone back into his pocket and leaned back in his seat, the city now looming large before him. The night was just beginning, and Zay knew that by the time it was over, the world would never be the same.

Draven's legacy would be written in blood, and Zay would be there to witness it all. Meanwhile Steve and the others were drunk. Lamar got up and left to go to his room and put on the outfit and Draven mask and pick up the axe and was looking for the captain.

Tom was smoking weed downstairs. He was high.

Lamar was walking down the stairs. Tom said, "What is this?" and started laughing. "Captain, is that you? This is no game. Stop playing and take off that mask!" Lamar was getting closer. Tom said really stop playing, take that damn mask off you blowing my high. Lamar raised his axe and chopped his head off.

Lamar picked up the head and tossed it in the water Lamar was looking for some more victims. And kill five more people. Lamar finds the captain and kills him. As the boat stopped, a low groan echoed through the ship.

Steve and Faith paused their conversation. Steve narrowed his eyes, turning to Faith with a look of concern. "Did you hear that?" He asked, his voice slightly slurred from the alcohol. But, his tone showed worry.

Faith furrowed her brow, trying to listen over the laughter and music filling the cruise deck. "I didn't hear anything... maybe it's just the engine?" she said, trying to dismiss the feeling of unease growing in the pit of her stomach.

Jade and the others were gathered, laughing and chatting. They were oblivious to the subtle shift in the atmosphere. "Steve, you're drunk. Relax," Jade called out, waving her hand dismissively. But Steve wasn't convinced. He stood up, wobbling slightly as he regained his balance.

"No, something's not right.

Where's Lamar?" He scanned the crowd, realizing Lamar had been missing for a while now. A cold chill settled over him as he recalled Lamar's strange behavior earlier that night. Meanwhile, deep in the ship, Lamar, now Draven, stalked the empty hallways. His breathing was slow and steady beneath the mask. The cold metal of the axe in his hand gleamed under the dim lights. Blood stained the weapon, dripping in a slow rhythm as he moved.

Lamar had already claimed six lives. Tom's headless body lay crumpled on the lower deck. The captain's lifeless form slumped in his office chair, eyes wide with terror. Lamar had severed communication lines, ensuring no distress calls could be made. The boat was trapped, just as Draven had planned.

Upstairs, the mood remained light, unaware of the bloodbath unfolding below. Lamar moved with purpose, his footsteps silent on the plush carpet as he made his way back up. The screams he craved the chaos wasn't far off now. Steve left the group and headed toward the lower decks. His gut told him something was wrong, and he was never one to ignore his instincts. He descended the stairs, passing by the lower lounge where Tom had been. The lights flickered ominously, and the smell of smoke and blood hung in the air.

Steve froze, his gaze locking onto a pool of blood seeping out from under a door. His heart pounded as he approached. He opened the door. It revealed a gruesome sight: Tom's headless body slumped in a chair, blood splattered on the walls. Steve's stomach churned as bile rose in his throat. He stumbled back, eyes wide with disbelief, trying to make sense of what he was seeing. "What the Hell!"

A shadow moved at the end of the hall. Steve turned around, his pulse quickening as he caught sight of a figure in a familiar mask, Draven mask. Steve ran upstairs as he made it to the top of the stairs Faith said what happened are you okay Steve said it's him. He is on the boat Draven is going to kill us all, Darnell, Faith, and the others turned to him in disbelief. Raven stood frozen, her face drained of color as Steve's words sank in. "What do you mean, Draven?" Darnell asked, trying to keep calm despite the tension crackling through the air. "Draven's dead."

"I saw him!" Steve insisted, panic in his eyes. "He's downstairs, wearing that mask killing people. Tom's dead. He's hunting us." Faith gripped Steve's arm, shaking him. "Are you sure it was Draven? What about Lamar? Where is he?" Steve's voice lowered. "I don't know where Lamar is. But I know what I saw. Draven is on this ship, and we have to get out of here now." Nia gasped, her hand flying to her mouth. "Lamar... What if he's wearing the mask? What if it's him?" Her voice trembled, fear creeping into her tone. "He's been acting strange all night." Steve said he was probably wearing his cousin's mask trying to scare us. Naomi said that's impossible.

Did the FBI get the mask? Jade said yea they supposed to have it right Steve said yeah you right but where in the hell is Lamar. We need to find Lamar," Darnell said, his mind racing as he tried to make sense of the horror unfolding around them. "If he's gone rogue, we have to stop him. We can't let this turn into a massacre." Meanwhile, Draven's followers got off the bus. They broke into houses and killed the innocents. Zay picked up a Rocket launcher and launched it inside an apartment. Everyone heard that.

Everyone got up and checked every nose. They saw someone's apartment on fire. So, they called the police.

The police called Kai. Kai Said we are on our way.

Every cop and the FBI went to the town in big trucks. Kai went outside, got in a truck and drove off. Jerry got up from the bed and left the hospital. He was going to the cruise ship. Draven made it to the doc and got on a boat to the same cruise ship. As Draven approached the ship, the dark waters lapped at its side. It was the only sound in the eerie silence. His boat glided silently through the waves. The moonlight reflected off the metallic mask that was now his new identity. He was getting closer, and the chaos he had planned was about to unfold.

Meanwhile, back in the city, Zay's madness continued. Draven's followers had broken into countless homes. The air filled with the sounds of destruction and death. Zay stood in the city's heart. He grinned as he watched his bombed apartment building burn. The flames danced, casting shadows over the city like a beacon of the terror they were spreading. Screams and sirens filled the air. People ran, terrified, from Draven's army's massacre.

Zay looked at the destruction and lit a blunt, taking a slow drag before flicking the match into the fire. The police were coming, but it was already too late. His work was done, and the city would remember this night as the beginning of Draven's reign of terror. When Kai arrived, Zay told everyone to choose. "If you want to go, go. If you want to stay, stay and fight." Most got on the bus and left. Only five stayed. When the buses left, Zay pushed a button and they exploded. Kai said, "Wow. You killed your own people. You tricked us all.

You're showing your true colors. I will kill you myself, Zay." Zay asked the five who stayed what their names were. They said, "Alicia, Kingston, Harry, Maxwell, Scarlett." Zay said, "Y'all will make history tonight." Kingston says, "Let's go. Let's kill the cops and FBI." Zay stood amidst the wreckage, his blunt hanging from his lips. The faint glow of its tip cast shadows on his face.

"Kai!" he called, his voice taunting, echoing across the battlefield of death and destruction. "You're too late! You and your team of heroes can't stop what's already been set in motion. Draven's plan is unstoppable. And this city will burn because of it." Kai stepped forward, his gun drawn, but his mind was clouded with fury. "You've betrayed everyone, Zay. Even your own people. You've become nothing more than a monster, just like Draven." Zay laughed, a twisted sound that grated on Kai's nerves. "A monster? No, Kai. I'm a visionary. And tonight, I'm going to show you just how wrong you are." Without warning, Zay raised his axe and charged at Kai. A primal scream tore from his throat. His followers moved with him. They drew their weapons and rushed the police and FBI agents who had come to stop them.

Kai sidestepped Zay's first strike, but Zay was fast, fueled by adrenaline and madness. The axe whistled through the air, narrowly missing Kai's head. "This ends now!" Kai shouted, firing a shot that grazed Zay's shoulder, but the man barely flinched. Zay swung again, this time with more precision, but Kai blocked it with a tactical shield. Alicia and the others charged at Kai's team. Metal clashed and guns fired as chaos erupted on the streets of the burning city.

Meanwhile, Jerry is on a boat on the way to the cruise. Back on the cruise ship, Steve and the others huddled together, desperately trying to come up with a plan. "We need weapons," Steve said, his voice shaky but determined. "Something to defend ourselves. We can't just wait here for him to kill us all."

"Where can we go?" Jade asked, looking around. "We're stuck in the middle of the ocean. There's nowhere to run." Darnell spoke up. "We need to find the ship's security room. If we regain control, we might send a distress signal.

Or, we could find a way to communicate with the mainland." Steve nodded. "And maybe we can track Lamar's movements with the security cameras. If we know where he is, we stand a chance."

The group agreed, though fear hung heavy in the air.

Together, they made their way through the dimly lit hallways, every sound making them jump. As they neared the security room, the door was already ajar. Darnell pushed it open cautiously, and they stepped inside. Faith gasped. The security monitors were all smashed. Wires hung from the ceiling. It was clear that Lamar had been here and had done everything in his power to cut them off from help.

Steve clenched his fists. "We're on our own," he

muttered. Suddenly, a chilling laugh echoed down the hallway outside. "You can't hide from me," a voice called, dripping with malice. It was Lamar or Draven, now fully consumed by the madness. "I'll find you. One by one." Panic surged through the group.

"We need to move!" Darnell urged. "Now!" Meanwhile, on the ocean outside the ship, Draven himself was closing in. His small boat cut through the waves. His eyes gleamed with anticipation. Soon, he would join Lamar in his carnage. Together, they would ensure no one left the ship alive.

Back in the city, Kai was still locked in his fierce battle with Zay. The street was littered with the bodies of Zay's 3 fallen followers and Kai's 15 fallen teammates.

Zay told the other two to run and never return. You two carried the will of Draven, and the fires spread as smoke filled the air. Zay, wounded but still full of fight, swung his axe at Kai. But, Kai countered, delivering a blow that sent Zay stumbling backward.

"You won't win this," Kai growled. "Not while I'm still standing." Zay grinned, blood trickling down his face. "Maybe not. But by the time you realize what's happening on that cruise ship, it'll already be too late." Kai Look at his teammates and said we done here let's go to the cruise ship. Out of nowhere, Zay swung his axe one last time. It went through Kai's heart. One of Kai's teammates, Eric, shot Zay in the head.

Zay and Kai Fall on the ground. Eric is mad of what happened to Kai. Eric's hands trembled as he knelt beside Kai's lifeless body. Blood pooled beneath his friend and mentor. The street was littered with the bodies of fallen comrades. Fires still raged in the distance. Zay's motionless body lay nearby, his reign of terror finally ended with a bullet to the head. Eric's chest heaved with grief and rage, his mind clouded with disbelief.

They had won the battle, but at what cost? As the last echoes of gunfire faded into the night, Eric's phone buzzed. It was Jerry. Eric answered, his voice raw. "Jerry..." "Eric, what's going on?" Jerry's voice crackled through the phone. "I've been trying to reach Kai.

Where is he?"

Chapter 8
Blood and Horror

Eric swallowed hard, his voice shaking as he replied, "Kai's... dead, Jerry. Zay killed him. We're too late." A heavy silence hung in the air. Jerry finally spoke, his tone grim. "We can't let his death be in vain. Lamar and Draven are on that ship, and they're going to slaughter everyone. We need to stop them." Eric said we can't leave the civilians we need to help them. You should go Jerry said I'm already on the boat Eric said be safe Jerry.

I will, Jerry said, his voice steady despite the gravity of the situation. As he turned to leave, Eric's gaze lingered on his retreating figure, a mixture of fear and hope in his heart. The sound of distant explosions echoed through the air, jolting Eric into action. He knew that every second counted. He sprinted towards the emergency shelters, rallying any remaining personnel and civilians. His mind raced as he formulated a plan to evacuate and protect them.

Meanwhile, getting closer to the ship, Jerry navigated the chaos with a fierce resolve. He moved through the corridors with purpose. Each step brought him closer to Lamar and Draven. The fight ahead would be brutal, but he was determined to see it through. The fate of countless lives depended on his ability to stop them.

Back on shore, Eric coordinated the evacuation, his commands sharp and precise. The civilians, frightened but trusting, followed his lead. He knew that every decision he made would impact their survival.

The battle between hope and despair was unfolding on two fronts. One was on the chaotic ship. The other was a desperate struggle to save lives on the ground. Both Jerry and Eric were racing against time, driven by a shared goal to prevent further tragedy. Meanwhile, on the ship, Jade and the others saw dead bodies everywhere. At least, it was over ten. Steve saw him again. It was Lamar, walking towards them. Jade asked, "Is that you, Lamar?"

Lamar did not answer and kept walking towards them. Darnell told everybody to go upstairs. Everyone was running upstairs. Nia said, are we going to die? Steve said no this dies tonight evil dies tonight Draven and Lamar dies tonight. I am not scared anymore. Let's kill them or kill him. Faith says we need some weapons. Steve went to his room and got his suitcase and put his suitcase on the bed and opened it. Steve's heart raced. He stared at the open suitcase. A bunch of guns gleamed in the dim light.

Faith and Nia were right, this was a small arsenal, more than enough to fight back. Steve grabbed a shotgun and tossed smaller handguns to the others. "This ends tonight," he muttered, loading the shotgun with practiced speed. "Lamar or Draven whoever they are now they don't get to leave this ship alive." Faith picked up a handgun, her hands shaking as she tried to steady herself. "Are we really going to do this?"

Steve met her eyes, his expression hardened with resolve. "We have no choice. We're not dealing with the Lamar we knew. Whoever he is now, he's a monster." Nia and Darnell nodded grimly, each grabbing a weapon from the case. The tension in the room was thick, the reality of what they were about to face sinking in. They had no idea what kind of fight awaited them, but they knew they had to be ready for anything.

Meanwhile, Lamar, now Draven, continued his slow, menacing approach up the stairs. His movements were eerily calm, deliberate, like a predator stalking its prey.

Blood still dripped from his axe, leaving a trail as he ascended. The hollow eyes of the Draven mask glinted in the flickering lights. His breathing was slow and controlled, as if savoring the moment before the kill. But No one had found out that it was five FBI agents on the ship hiding, waiting for the right time to take down Draven. Back on the boat Jerry sped toward the cruise ship, the boat cutting through the water at a blistering pace. The distant glow of flames from the ship's deck made Jerry's heart pound with urgency. He felt the weight of everything on his shoulders. Kai's death. The loss of innocent lives. Now, the impending massacre on the ship. Lamar cut off the power and the back of generators came on, so it was kind of dark. Imani and Raven, huddled in fear, exchanged worried glances.

The lights flickered again. "What is that?" Imani whispered, her voice trembling as she pointed toward a shadow moving at the far end of the corridor. Darnell squinted through the dim light, his heart hammering in his chest. "It's a shadow... but it's moving." Suddenly, without warning, Darius bolted, his body propelled by pure fear. The rest of the group followed in a blind panic, sprinting up the stairs as fast as their legs could carry them. But Steve and Darnell held their ground. Steve's hand tightened around his shotgun's grip as he aimed at the moving figure. His finger twitched on the trigger.

"Stay back!" Steve yelled, his voice echoing through the hallway. The shadowy figure paused, then moved again, faster and more aggressively. Darnell, trembling, raised his handgun and started firing wildly. The muzzle flashes briefly lit the figure. It revealed the glint of the Draven mask. Lamar or what was left of him was advancing toward them, seemingly unfazed by the gunfire. His movements were steady, slow but unstoppable, like death itself. Steve and Darnell said, "Hell naw!" Then, they ran with the group at the back of the boat. Everyone had guns pointed at the shadow.

Steve said, "Come out, Lamar!" Draven walked out of the shadows. Jade asked, "What did you do with Lamar?" Darius said "Ain't that's Lamar we all were thinking that he was gone for a very long time and we still can't find him. That is so suspicious Jade said you are just drunk Darius. Steve said but he got to a point where Lamar is at this point. We should've seen his body. Lamar took off the mask. Darnell said you killed my brother, I'm gonna kill you. Lamar said you killed my cousins, my only family in this world. Steve said calm down. Darnell pushed Steve out the way and started shooting Lamar. You are a lazy shooter as he walked forward blocking all the shots with his axe.

Out of nowhere, the five FBI agents came out and said put your hands up. You kill enough people today it's time for you to go to jail. Lamar started to laugh and said you can put me in jail. Nobody is leaving this boat.

Everybody is dying. Do you understand Lamar Reach for three blades through it at three FBI agents? The three FBI agents fell on the ground and the other two shot Lamar and Faith shot him seven times in the chest. Lamar fell down face first. The two FBI agents asked, "Is everybody okay?" Steve replied, "We're good." One of the agents tried to shoot the mask. Out of nowhere, Draven stabbed him in the back with his blade. Faith took out her phone and started recording.

Draven lifted him and threw him off the ship. As Draven walked to his mask, tension grew. Now wearing it, he loomed over the ship. His aura radiated with a dark, suffocating malevolence. It crushed all around him. He walked slowly but with resolve. He savored the terror rippling through the survivors.

Faith, with trembling hands, clutched her phone and recorded. Her breath hitched as Draven approached the fallen FBI agent. His mask glinted ominously in the dim light. It hid any humanity that might have existed beneath it. The axe's sickening, slicing sound filled the air. With each brutal swing, the FBI agent's blood stained the deck. Ten vicious strikes, each more forceful than the last. The body was a crumpled, unrecognizable heap.

Blood spattered across the walls and floor. It was a grotesque display of Draven's raw power and sadistic control. Steve and Darnell watched in horror, frozen in place. Their bodies, already weakened by fear and fatigue, felt heavier in Draven's presence. The weight of his aura pressed down on them like an invisible force, making it hard to breathe. Imani, Nia, and

Darius collapsed. They could not bear Draven's oppressive energy. Their bodies hit the deck with dull thuds, eyes wide with terror as they struggled to stay conscious.

Steve, shaking but defiant, finally spoke, his voice hoarse. "I knew it. I knew you were never dead. I had a feeling all along..." Draven turned his masked face toward Steve. His gaze pierced the mask's hollow eye sockets. There was no response, no acknowledgment of Steve's words. Draven didn't need to speak. His silence was a far more terrifying answer. He raised his axe, the blood still dripping from its blade, and took a slow step toward Steve. Darnell, feeling the crushing pressure of Draven's aura, gasped, "What the hell is happening? It's like... like he's controlling us somehow..." "It's his aura," Steve replied, his voice barely above a whisper. "He has perfect control over it.

It's like he's draining our will, our strength."

Draven stood over them now, a silent figure of death. His grip tightened around the handle of the axe, and the world seemed to slow to a crawl. Every breath was labored, every heartbeat a painful reminder of how close they were to the end. Faith's phone slipped from her hands and banged to the ground. She stared up at Draven, paralyzed by his overwhelming presence. The video feed kept recording. It captured the final moments of their last stand. Steve, summoning what little courage he had left, met Draven's gaze. "You might have us now... but this ends tonight. One way or another, your reign of terror ends."

Draven tilted his head slightly, as if considering Steve's words. Then, without a word, he raised the axe high above his head, preparing to bring it down on Steve. Time seemed to stand still as Steve braced himself for the blow.

But before the axe could fall, a sudden sound cut through the heavy air, a loud blast from a ship's horn. Draven paused, turning his head toward the source of the noise. Jerry had arrived. His boat smashed against the side of the cruise ship, and the sound of the impact repeated through the shell. Steve and the others that were still up run.

In the distance, sirens could be heard approaching. Reinforcements. Draven turned back to Steve, but they were gone. Those on the ground got up and began to shoot at him. He threw his axe at Dauris' heart. Nia's scream echoed across the deck. She tried to flee, her panicked eyes searching for an escape. But Draven was too fast. With one swift move, he seized her by the neck. He lifted her off the ground with a single hand. Nia struggled, kicking and clawing at Draven's arm, but his grip was unstoppable, like steel.

Steve and the others watched, helpless, as the scene unfolded in horrific slow motion. Their hearts pounded in their chests. Darnell tried to move, to act, but the pure force of Draven's aura made him feel like he was trapped in quicksand. His limbs wouldn't obey.

Nia's voice, once so full of terror, was choked out as Draven's grip tightened around her throat. With a cold, deliberate motion, he snapped her neck. The sickening crack echoed louder than any scream or chaos. Her body went limp, and Draven let her fall to the blood-soaked deck without a second glance.

Imani, frozen in fear, turned to run, but her foot slipped in the thick pool of blood on the floor. She crashed onto the deck. Her hands splattered in the crimson mess.

She tried, in vain, to push herself up. Tears streamed down her face as she crawled. Her hands trembled as she sought refuge. But, her panic made it impossible to move fast enough. Draven walked toward Imani and stabbed her in the neck. Jerry leaped from the boat onto the deck of the cruise ship, his gun drawn. His eyes locked onto Draven, filled with fury and determination. "It ends tonight, Draven," Jerry snarled, his voice steady and cold. Draven remained still, his masked face unreadable. But there was no mistaking the tension in the air. The final showdown had begun.

Steve said let's Jump him. My mama always said one fight we all fight. Darnell, filled with adrenaline and rage, turned to Raven. His voice was low but intense. "Let me kill him. After we jump him, I'll finish it."

Raven, still catching her breath and wiping the blood from her hands, nodded grimly. "Okay," she whispered. Her eyes narrowed as she sized up Draven. He stood like an unstoppable force in front of them. Jade, trembling but resolute, stepped forward. "We have to be smart about this," she said, her voice shaking but determined. "We can't just rush him. He's too strong.

We need to distract him from something to get the upper hand."

Steve wiped the sweat from his forehead. His eyes darted around for a weapon, or anything to catch Draven off guard. "Darnell's right. We can't run anymore. We take him down here, or none of us make it off this boat alive." Faith, clutching a broken piece of glass she had found on the floor, looked at the others. "We've got one shot. We either all hit him at once, or he kills us all, one by one."

Imani, still shaking from her fall, got to her feet. A steely determination settled in her eyes. "Let's do this," she said, though fear still flickered in her voice. Draven, unaware of their plotting, continued his slow, menacing advance. He gripped his blood-stained axe. His breath echoed through the mask. He was savoring the fear, the tension, and the chaos. Jerry shot at Draven and Draven blocked the bullets with his axe then went downstairs. Meanwhile, Eric and his team searched the land. They worked tirelessly to find the last two members of Draven's crew.

Chapter 9
Blood on the Deck

Scarlett and Kingston were on a boat to Draven. Back on the ship, Jerry, Steve, and the others were preparing for what seemed like their last stand. The tension was thick as they made their way down the blood-streaked stairs after Draven. They heard the faint clank of his axe as he went below deck. His slow, deliberate footsteps sent chills down their spines.

Jerry signaled for the others to spread out. "We're gonna need to corner him, surround him from all sides. He's strong, but he's not invincible." He looked at Steve and the group. "We do this together, or we don't do it at all." Darnell said, "That's white people stuff. Jerry, you're black. Stop saying white things." Steve stepped in. "I know, but this is the only way to kill Draven." Jerry said are y'all ready Steve nodded, his face hard with determination. "Let's end this."

They split into two groups. Each crept down the narrow stairwells. The ship's hull creaked with every step.

Below deck, the dim lights flickered, casting eerie shadows across the hallway. The sound of the ocean was distant, drowned out by the slow, deliberate steps of their pursuer.

Draven stopped in the center of the lower deck, standing among the rows of cabins. The air felt heavy, thick with the smell of death and saltwater. He swung his axe lazily, tapping the floor with it as if daring them to come closer. His mask gleamed in the dim light, a soul of terror, and behind it. Lamar got up and removed the bulletproof vest under his clothes. Then, he walked to his room to get his bow and arrow and began to search for Draven.

Meanwhile back at the hospital Isaiah woke up and said where I am? I can't feel my legs. A doctor came in and said you were in a coma for some months and a killer cut your legs off with an axe. Isaiah said where is Jerry? A doctor said he left Isaiah to grab his phone and call Jerry. But, he wasn't picking up. So, he tried to call Kai, but he didn't answer either. So, he called Eric.

Eric answered the phone. He said, "You woke up. It's about time. You've been in a coma for months." Isaiah replied, "The doctors told me. So, what's going on? I called Kai and Jerry, but they didn't pick up."

Eric said, "Slow down. Kai is dead and Jerry is on the ship." Isaiah asked, "What about Zay? He put me in the hospital." Eric replied, "I was just going to tell you. Zay killed Kai. One of our team killed Zay." Isaiah asked, "What else happened while I was in a coma?" Eric said, "A lot. The group's parents are dead. We think Draven and Zay did it. They mailed a package to each house and blew them up. Then, they broke into a crazy place, freed everybody, and made them kill for them. Zay will kill anyone who went back on the bus. We have the FBI, NCIS, CIA, and CSI on the case."

Isaiah said damn I will let you go I'm going to get some rest because I still feel sore. Eric said ok we got this covered evil dies tonight Draven dies tonight. And the phone hung up. Isaiah lay back on the hospital bed, trying to process everything Eric had just told him. His mind was racing, but his body was weak, sore, and incomplete. The news of Kai's death, Jerry on the ship, and Zay and Draven's destruction weighed heavily on his chest. He had been out of commission for months, and in that time, everything had fallen apart.

His legs were gone. Zay had done this to him, but now Zay was dead. It should've brought him some satisfaction, but all Isaiah felt was emptiness and rage.

His hands trembled as he set the phone down on the bedside table. He was powerless, stuck in this hospital bed. His friends were out there, risking their lives.

Isaiah's eyes flickered to the door, the beeping of the heart monitor steady beside him. He needed to do something. Lying here wasn't an option. He exhaled sharply. "Not like this," he muttered under his breath. "I won't let it end like this."

But first, rest. His body demanded it, and his mind was too overloaded to resist. Isaiah closed his eyes, hoping that sleep would bring clarity, or at least a moment of peace. Eric knelt, pressing his hands into the dirt. He felt the weight of everything that had just unfolded.

Bodies of the fallen lay around him, both enemies and allies. The acrid scent of smoke and blood still lingered in the air. The ground beneath him felt cold and damp, soaked with the aftermath of battle. He could hear distant sirens wailing. Help was coming. But, the weight of the situation rested heavily on his shoulders.

"All of Draven's forces are dead," Eric muttered, looking at the few remaining soldiers who had survived. "But two more of his soldiers are still out there. We can't let them regroup. We have to finish this." A few feet away, Agent Harris spoke into his radio. He was coordinating the medical units and the evacuation plan for the injured. "We're getting the wounded to the hospital," he called over to Eric. "But we need to know our next move."

Eric rose to his feet, wiping the blood and sweat from

his face. He turned to the FBI and NCIS agents who had arrived in the aftermath. Their grim faces told him they knew the seriousness of the situation.

"We need to act fast," Eric said, his voice steady but urgent. But we still have three more threats out there. Zay's gone, but those two... they're going to regroup, and when they do, they'll be even more dangerous. We need to track them down before they can strike again." One of the FBI agents, a woman with sharp eyes and a no-nonsense demeanor, stepped forward. "We're working on it," she said. "We've got a perimeter set up, and teams are already searching the area. But we need Intel. Do you have anything on their whereabouts?" Eric shook his head. "They disappeared during the fight.

They're smart, and they know how to vanish when things get tight. But we can't let them get too far." Agent Harris stepped closer, lowering his radio. "What about the civilians? What's the status there?"

Eric sighed heavily. "There are injured civilians still here. We need to prioritize them, get them to safety first. But we can't take our eyes off the remaining threats. If we don't deal with those three soon, they'll come back even more prepared." "I agree," Harris said. "We need to split our resources. I'll handle getting the injured out and coordinating with the hospitals. But you need to work with the FBI and

NCIS to figure out where these last threats went." Eric nodded, his mind already racing with possibilities. He turned to the FBI agent again. "We need to coordinate a full-scale manhunt.

They can't have gone far. With all the chaos, they might try to lay low for now, but they'll be back, and we need to be ready." The agent nodded. "We'll start by scouring the surrounding areas. But we'll need your help. You know them better than anyone." "I'm in," Eric said, his tone firm. "We've come too far to let them escape. This ends tonight." He glanced around at the battlefield again. So much destruction, so much loss. But there was no time to dwell on it. Innocent people were still in danger, and they had a job to do.

"I'll gather the team," Eric said, stepping toward the remaining fighters. "We need to prepare for the worst." As he moved, Eric's mind was laser-focused on the task ahead. There was no time for hesitation. Draven's reign of terror had to end, and Eric would do everything in his power to make sure of it. But the question that lingered in the back of his mind was simple: would it be enough? Meanwhile, Lamar creeps through the dimly lit ship's halls. His movements are silent, and his senses are heightened.

The bow and arrow he carried felt heavy in his hands. But, it wasn't their weight that burdened him. It was the knowledge of the final act that was coming.

Draven was still out there. He was planning something big. It would plunge their world into darker chaos. Lamar's heartbeat quickened as he neared the ship's front. He was getting closer to his target.

He paused for a moment, listening. Footsteps. Faint, but unmistakable. Lamar ducked behind a steel pillar, peering around the corner. His eyes narrowed as he spotted Draven standing at the far end of the deck. He watched Draven at the far end of the deck. The ship's darkness improved every sound. The floorboards creaked. Waves crashed against the hull. Muffled cries came from those hiding, desperate to survive the night.

He knew Draven was dangerous, perhaps the most dangerous opponent he had ever faced. But there was something different about him tonight. Something more savage, more deliberate. Lamar watched Draven. He moved with deadly precision. His axe swung methodically as he hunted anyone who crossed his path. A dark, twisted partnership. That's what this was.

Lamar had fought alongside Draven. They wanted to destroy the corrupt system that killed innocent crew. "Focus," Lamar whispered, shaking off the doubt. He knew what he had to do. He had to help Draven complete their mission. They were so close, and the world needed to see that those in power weren't untouchable. But the killing, the bloodshed have to leave a mark. Lamar stepped out of the shadow and said hi Draven let's start the final phase. I already planted a boom around the ship and I spread the gasoline on the lower deck. Draven's eyes widened slightly, but he didn't say a word. He just stared at Lamar, his grip tightening on the axe. For a moment, the two men stood in silence, the tension between them palpable.

Lamar took a deep breath, his fingers grazing the bowstring, but he kept his gaze steady on Draven. "It's all set," he continued, his voice steady despite the pounding of his heart. "Just waiting for your signal."

Still, Draven didn't speak. His eyes flicked to the survivors, huddled together in fear, then back to Lamar. His silence was unnerving, but Lamar held his ground.

Lamar forced a smile, though it felt strained and hollow. "I know this was part of the plan," he said, trying to keep his tone light, "but I thought we could make a real statement. Something they can't ignore."

Draven's jaw clenched, his eyes narrowing as he studied Lamar. There was something dangerous in his gaze, a cold fury simmering beneath the surface. But he still didn't say a word. Lamar's heart raced.

Draven's silence was more terrifying than any words he could have spoken. He took a step closer, lowering his voice. "We have to do this together, Draven. It's the only way." Draven's lips pressed into a thin line, his eyes never leaving Lamar's. The silence stretched on, heavy and oppressive. It made it hard for Lamar to breathe. "Say something," Lamar whispered, his voice barely more than a breath. "Tell me this is what you want." Draven remained still, his eyes cold and unreadable then he nodded. Lamar said great let's make our way upstairs.

Draven followed silently. His axe, stained with blood, hung ominously from his grip. Lamar was in the middle of the ship, screaming, "Where are you?" The dimly lit hallway felt eerie as Steve, Faith, Darnell, and the rest of the group caught their breath. They had just survived a brutal fight, and it seemed like everything was over.

Faith looked down at her hands, which were still covered in blood. She had shot Lamar herself, and he should have been dead.

"I killed him," Faith whispered, still in disbelief. She looked at Steve, her eyes wide with confusion. "Why do I still hear his voice?" Steve nodded, his own face pale. "Me too. It's like he's still here, watching us." Darnell stood nearby, gripping his gun tightly. His heart pounded in his chest, and his mind raced with fear. "We all saw him go down, right? He can't still be alive." The group exchanged nervous glances, their fear growing.

The ship groaned and creaked around them, as if it were alive, adding to the tension that hung thick in the air. Steve took a deep breath, trying to calm himself, but the strange whispers in his mind wouldn't stop.

Every time the ship creaked, it felt like Draven was right there with them. Jerry said stop, let's make a plan "Stop. We need to make a plan," he said, his voice calm but firm.

The others turned toward him, their panic momentarily paused. Jerry looked at each of them, trying to steady his own nerves. "We can't keep running around like this. If Draven or Lamar, whoever it is, is still alive, we need to think this through." Faith wiped her hands on her pants, her whole body trembling. "What plan? I shot him. He's dead." Jerry shook his head. "I don't know what's happening either, but we can't assume anything right now. Something is messing with us, but we need to stay focused."

Darnell nodded slowly. "So, what do we do? If they're still out there..." Jerry's eyes hardened. He glanced at the rest of the group: Faith, Steve, Darnell, Raven,

Jade, and Naomi, who had just caught up to them. "We fight. We're black, and we shouldn't be hiding from killers. We fight back." They went upstairs.

Chapter 10
Blood and Ashes

Meanwhile, back on shore, Eric and his team finished cleaning up the bloodbath. Eric said, "Let's get a helicopter. We need to get to that ship now." The FBI gave a helicopter to them. Eric gets in the Helicopter before they left. Eric said we will see you there. The FBI and CSI agent said we are right behind you.

Scarlett and Kingston are getting close to Draven. The helicopter's blades roared, slicing through the night.

Eric and his team hovered over the dark ocean. The ship loomed ahead like a ghostly silhouette. A faint orange glow flickered in the distance. It was from gasoline-soaked decks. Draven was somewhere on that ship, and they had to stop him before everything went up in flames.

Eric's mind raced as the helicopter drew closer to the deck. The air was thick and suffocating with tension.

His team prepared for what felt like a final confrontation. He was haunted by the memories of their fallen comrades. Draven's reign of terror had ruined many lives. "Hold on," Eric muttered as the helicopter began to descend, his knuckles white as he gripped his weapon. "We're almost there."

As the helicopter touched down with a heavy thud,

Eric and his team sprang into action. The FBI agents, following closely behind, moved with precision. Their weapons were drawn and their eyes sharp. They knew they had no time to waste. Gasoline fumes filled the air.

The explosives Lamar had planted could ignite at any moment. "Fan out," Eric ordered, his voice cutting through the chaos. "We need to find Jerry and the others before it's too late." They moved swiftly, their eyes darting to the gasoline on the lower deck. It reeked of impending destruction. The dull creaks of the ship groaned beneath their feet, amplifying the tension. Suddenly, a dark silhouette emerged from the shadows near the bow of the ship. It was Lamar. His eyes gleamed with madness, and in his hand, gripped tightly, was the detonator. "Lamar! Don't do it!" Eric yelled, his weapon trained on him. "This doesn't have to end like this!" For a fleeting moment, Lamar hesitated. His fingers hovered over the button. His eyes flicked from Eric to the remaining survivors on the deck: Jerry, Faith, Steve, and the others. But then his face twisted into a wicked grin. "This is what it was always supposed to be," Lamar growled. His voice, though calm, was soaked in malice. "A final statement." Before Eric or anyone could react, Lamar's thumb pressed the detonator. Time seemed to slow as Eric's heart sank. "No!" he screamed, but it was too late.

The ship erupted in a deafening explosion. A fiery blast tore through the hull, the force of it throwing bodies into the air like ragdolls. Flames engulfed the deck, the gasoline catching instantly, spreading fire in every direction. The shockwave slammed Eric against the helicopter's side. It was caught in the firestorm's upward thrust. Jerry, Steve, Faith, Darnel everyone scattered, thrown by the explosion's sheer force. The inferno's roar drowned the screams. Metal groaned and cracked as the ship split apart in the heat. The sky turned a blistering orange as fire licked the night air.

Eric's head spun as he fought to stay conscious, blood trickling from a gash on his forehead. His ears rang from the explosion, and the acrid smell of smoke and burning metal filled his lungs. "Jerry!" he screamed, trying to get to his feet, but his body felt heavy, sluggish.

In the midst of the chaos, Jerry struggled to lift himself from the wreckage. Blood dripped from a gash above his eye. His vision blurred, but he could make out the ship's twisted remains around him. Flames danced in every direction, and the ship was sinking fast. "Steve Faith" Jerry coughed, his throat raw from the smoke. His eyes scanned the wreckage, searching for any sign of his friends. But all he could see was fire, debris, and death. Steve staggered up from a pile of debris nearby, his clothes singed, but he was alive. "Jerry! Over here!" he yelled, waving him down. Beside him, Faith and Darnell groaned. They tried to free themselves from the rubble. "We've got to get out of here!" Steve shouted.

"This ship's going down!" Jerry nodded, adrenaline pumping through his veins. They had to move, but everything was a blur. In the distance, Eric and his team were struggling to reach them, but the fire was closing in fast. The ship tilted as the flames consumed the deck. The air filled with the sound of metal tearing apart. The once mighty vessel was now a sinking, burning tomb. Suddenly, from the heart of the flames, Draven stood at the ship's top. The fire consumed the lower decks, casting an eerie glow on the wreckage.

His axe rested at his side, its blade still dripping with the blood of those who had fallen before him. He showed no panic. Only cold, calculating patience. He waited for the perfect moment to strike.

The ship groaned beneath his feet, teetering on the edge of collapse, but Draven was unfazed. His eyes were fixed on the dark waters below, scanning for any sign of Eric or the others. He knew they were coming for him—he could feel it. This was where it would all end.

Jerry, Steve, Faith, and Darnell fought to the top deck.

The explosion and chaos below had battered their bodies. Flames roared around them, but they pressed on, determined to end Draven's reign of terror once and for all. The group's faces were streaked with ash and blood, but their eyes burned with determination.

As they reached the top, they stopped dead in their tracks. Lamar was standing there, his back to them, the detonator still clutched in his hand. His body swayed slightly, weakened by the fight and the blast. But, he remained defiant. The ship was moments away from going down, yet Lamar stood there, like a man waiting for his moment of glory. Jerry's heart pounded in his chest. "Lamar!" he shouted, stepping forward despite the fear rising inside him. "It's over!" This ship is doomed, and Draven's plan stops here!"" Lamar turned slowly, his face a twisted mix of anger and madness.

His eyes gleamed with an unsettling calm. "You think it's over, Jerry?" he hissed, his voice barely above a whisper. "You have no idea what's coming." Jerry tightened his grip on his weapon, his voice steady. "We're taking Draven down. You can't stop that now." Lamar laughed, a chilling sound that sent shivers through the group. "Oh, I'm not stopping anything. I'm just... playing my part." Suddenly, the floor creaked.

The ship lurched, throwing everyone off balance. The group struggled to stay on their feet as the ship groaned, sinking further into the ocean. Lamar aimed his bow at their guns. Jerry ran to him, but Lamar pulled a blade and stabbed him in the back. Jerry had a grenade. Jerry's heart pounded as he rushed to Lamar's fallen body, driven by rage and desperation.

With a final, painful lunge, Jerry hauled Lamar over the railing with him. Both men plummeted into the dark waters below. The freezing ocean swallowed them. For a split second, there was only the cold and the deep silence of the water enveloping them. Then the explosion. A loud boom ripped through the air, sending a shockwave across the surface of the water. The force of the grenade's blast shot a column of water high into the sky, mixed with bits of debris and blood. The ship shook from the power of the explosion, and for a moment, everything went still. Back on the deck, Steve, Faith, and Darnell froze, their hearts sinking as they heard the explosion. They knew Jerry was gone. He had taken Lamar with him. In a final act of bravery, he took Lamar with him. He sacrificed himself to ensure Lamar would never hurt anyone again Jerry opened the grenade and they blew up in the water.

"Jerry..." Faith whispered, tears filling her eyes. But there was no time to mourn, not yet. Draven was still out there. Meanwhile, on the lower deck, Eric and the remaining agents raced up the stairs. They echoed from Lamar's explosion. Their ears are still ringing. The whole ship felt unstable. The creaks and groans grew louder. The gasoline-soaked vessel was one spark away from igniting. Five minutes later, they burst onto the upper deck. Breathless, they scanned the chaos before them. Steve was standing there, his face pale and his eyes wide with the horror of what had just happened. "Where is Draven?" Eric demanded, scanning the deck with a growing sense of urgency.

Steve shook his head, his voice hollow. "I don't know... Jerry just—Jerry's gone. He took Lamar with him." His voice cracked with emotion. "Jerry died for us." Eric's expression hardened. Jerry's sacrifice weighed heavily on him. There was no time to grieve, not yet. "We have to find Draven. This isn't over. Not until he's dead." Suddenly, two FBI agents who had been keeping watch nearby stiffened. A dark presence loomed behind them, casting an ominous shadow on the deck.

Eric's blood ran cold as his eyes locked onto Draven. He stood directly behind the two agents. His face was twisted in that same, eerie, calm expression. A large axe hung loosely from his hand. Eric's heart pounded in his chest as he realized the danger. "Behind you!"

Eric shouted, his voice filled with desperation. But it was already too late. Draven moved faster than anyone could react. In one swift, brutal motion, his hands shot forward like iron claws. He plunged them deep into the agents' backs. His fingers tore through their flesh with horrifying precision. The agents gasped, their bodies going rigid as Draven's hands pierced their chests.

Blood splattered across the deck as Draven's fingers closed around their hearts. He gripped the still-beating organs tightly. Their eyes widened in shock and terror as they tried to scream, but no sound escaped. Eric and the others watched in horror as Draven, with a sickening smile, yanked his hands back. He pulled out both hearts with a grotesque squelch. Blood dripped from his fingers, the hearts still faintly beating in his grasp.

For a brief moment, he stood there, holding the agents' hearts in his hands as if they were trophies. Then, with deliberate cruelty, Draven squeezed. He crushed the organs in his fists until they were a bloody mess that dripped onto the deck. The agents' dead bodies crumpled at Draven's feet. Their eyes stared blankly into the void. "NO!" Steve screamed, rushing forward, but Jade grabbed him, holding him back. Eric stood frozen, his fists clenched, every muscle in his body tensing with rage. This monster, this force of death and destruction, had to be stopped. Draven turned his gaze to the rest of them, his dark mask gleaming with malice. Eric raised his weapon, locking eyes with Draven. "This ends now." Raven said why are you doing this, it's because we left you and your sister? Draven didn't respond. His towering, shadowy, blood-soaked form seemed to absorb the question. It showed no emotion.

His mask covered his face, but his silence was more menacing than any words he could've spoken.

Faith stepped forward, her heart racing, her voice breaking as she spoke. "We were just kids, Vontae. We didn't know… we didn't know you two were still in the house. If we had known…"

Chapter 11
Draven last stand

Her words trailed off, the weight of guilt and regret pressing down on her. "We were scared." Draven remained motionless, his silence suffocating, his eyes hidden behind the cold mask. His breathing was slow, deliberate, as if he was waiting for something. Or maybe he was savoring the moment. He let their words wash over him. He had no intention of giving them what they sought: a sign of understanding, or even hate.

Raven, her emotions raw, stepped closer. "Vontae, please. This isn't what she would have wanted. Your sister... she wouldn't want this! You're doing this for revenge, but it's not going to bring her back!" For a brief second, something flickered in Draven's stance. A twitch in his hand gripped the axe. But, he said nothing.

Eric, standing behind Raven and Faith, was gripping his gun tightly. "We don't have time for this," he muttered, his eyes never leaving Draven. "We need to take him down. Now." Draven's silence grew heavier. It became oppressive. He slowly raised his axe. The faint light caught its metallic gleam. Faith's eyes widened, her heart pounding in her chest. "Vontae, please! "You don't have to do this!" For the first time in years, Draven finally spoke. His voice was low and gravelly. It echoed through the tense silence like a blade slicing the air. "My name is Draven," he rasped, his tone cold, devoid of any warmth or humanity. The words sent chills down Raven and Faith's spines. "I'm not killing you for revenge... believe me, I've had my revenge."

Faith and Raven exchanged glances. Confusion grew as Draven continued, his grip on the axe tightening. His massive frame loomed over them like a shadow. "Something changed," he said slowly, his voice unnervingly calm. "I thought it was about vengeance... about making you all pay for what you did. For leaving us to die. But it's more than that now." He lifted his head slightly, the dim light glinting off his mask. Behind it, his cold, empty eyes flickered. They held a darker, twisted thing, more than anger.

"Something *told* me to kill. Everyone. Not just the ones who left me... but everyone who gets in my way."

Raven's breath caught in her throat, her heart hammering as she stared at him. "Draven, you don't have to listen to it," she pleaded, her voice shaking. "You're stronger than this. You were always stronger than us. This isn't you."

Draven's silence returned, more terrifying than ever.

His free hand clenched into a fist, as if he were struggling against something unseen. For a fleeting moment, his body language showed conflict. It was a struggle between the man he used to be and the monster he had become. But it passed in an instant, replaced by a chilling resolve. "It's too late," Draven growled, his voice dripping with finality. "This... is who I am now. The man you left behind is dead, just like my sister. I've become what I was always meant to be." Eric stepped forward, his gun aimed at Draven, his expression hard. "We're not letting you hurt anyone else, Draven," he said firmly, his finger hovering over the trigger. "This ends here." Draven tilted his head, his eerie mask gleaming in the faint light. "No, Eric," he said darkly. "This only ends when I'm finished." He raised his axe high above his head, ready to strike. At that moment, everything slowed. Raven and Faith screamed, and Eric's eyes widened as he pulled the trigger. As Eric fired, the bullet ricocheted off Draven's axe with a sharp clang, sparks flying in the dim light.

Draven stood tall, his axe raised high, glaring down at them with cold, unflinching eyes. He had become a force of pure destruction.

Steve, his mind racing, shouted over the chaos, "I have a plan! Jade, Raven, everyone listen up!" But before he could explain, Eric and his team couldn't wait any longer. The bloodshed before them demanded action.

Hesitation wasn't an option. Ignoring Steve's attempts to plan, Eric signaled his team. They charged forward, determined to bring down Draven. The first to strike was Agent Harris, his gun raised. He fired multiple rounds, but Draven's reflexes were lightning fast. With a smooth twist, Draven swung his axe. It deflected each bullet with bone-chilling precision. Sparks flew as the bullets ricocheted off the blade. Harris's eyes went wide as Draven closed the distance between them.

Before Harris could react, Draven was upon him. The axe came down with terrifying force. It sliced through Harris's gun and buried deep in his chest. Blood sprayed out in a gruesome arc as Harris fell to the floor, his body twitching in its final moments. Agent Johnson, the next in line, fired in desperation as she ran at Draven. Her bullets hit the walls and floor as she struggled to aim through her panic. Draven, showing no mercy, launched his axe in a brutal sideways swing.

The blade caught her mid-run, carving into her abdomen. She let out a guttural scream, dropping to her knees as her lifeblood pooled beneath her.

Eric, witnessing his teammates fall, roared in anger.

"Get away from them, you monster!" He sprinted toward Draven, grabbing a metal pipe from the deck as a makeshift weapon. He swung hard at Draven's head.

But, Draven easily ducked. Before Eric could react, Draven kicked him in the chest. He hit the metal walls with a hard thud.

Draven's methodical killing continued. Agent Ramirez leaped forward to flank him. But, Draven spun. His axe sliced the air like a predator's fang. The blade connected with Ramirez's leg, severing it below the knee in a gruesome spray of blood. Ramirez collapsed, screaming in agony. He clutched the gushing wound.

The light in his eyes began to fade. "One by one," Draven muttered under his breath, his voice cold and devoid of emotion. Eric, dazed but alive, forced himself to his feet. He could see his team, scattered on the deck like broken toys. Some were motionless, while others writhed in pain. His heart pounded, his mind racing as he stared into Draven's lifeless eyes.

Draven's axe, dripping with the blood of Eric's comrades, glinted in the dim light. He advanced slowly, ready to claim another life. But Eric, battered and bloody, refused to give in to fear. He gripped his pipe tightly, knowing this might be the last stand for him and his team. "We're not done yet," Eric growled.

He stepped forward, ready to face Draven in a last, desperate attempt to stop the monster. Draven dropped his bloodstained axe, its metallic clang echoing across the deck. Without his weapon, he turned his cold, dead eyes to Eric. Eric was already charging forward with a steel pipe. The two clashed violently, Eric swinging the pipe with all the strength he could muster. Draven dodged and weaved with deadly precision. His fists landed brutal punches between Eric's wild swings.

Eric managed to land a few hits, striking Draven's side and shoulder, but it seemed to barely faze him. Draven's right hook sent Eric staggering back, blood trickling from his mouth. But Eric didn't stop. Consumed by rage at his team's slaughter, he rushed forward. He slammed the pipe across Draven's ribs. The impact echoed with a dull thud, but Draven still didn't falter.

Instead, his face twisted into something darker, an expression that sent a chill down Eric's spine. In one swift move, Draven lunged. He grabbed Eric by the throat and lifted him off the ground. Eric gasped, his hands instinctively clawing at Draven's iron grip, but it was no use. Draven's strength was monstrous, inhuman. The pipe slipped from Eric's fingers, clattering uselessly on the floor. With a guttural growl, Draven shifted his grip, moving his massive hand to Eric's head. Eric's eyes widened in horror as he realized what was about to happen. He kicked and thrashed in a desperate attempt to break free, but Draven's grip only tightened. Draven's fingers dug into the sides of Eric's skull, and with a sickening crack, he twisted. Eric's body went limp, his neck snapping under the sheer force of Draven's grip. The body dropped to the deck with a hollow thud. Eric's eyes stared blankly into nothingness.

Draven stood there for a moment. His breath was slow and even, as if the brutal execution had been routine. He wiped the blood from his hands on his coat, turning to look at the rest of the ship. The bodies of his enemies littered the deck, and the air was thick with the stench of death and saltwater. Draven's mission was almost complete. Jade called Draven and said, "You are weak." Draven staggered, feeling the blade Jada had thrust into his ribs. Blood oozed from the wound, but it wasn't enough to stop him. His eyes locked on her with cold fury as he grabbed her in a brutal bear hug. Jada gasped for air, struggling against his iron grip, but Draven was relentless. His grip tightened. Her ribs cracked. The sound echoed as her body broke.

Before her last breath escaped her, Jade reached up, tearing the mask off Draven's face. She threw it toward Zuri, who caught it, her eyes wide with terror.

Draven's scarred and mangled face was revealed, twisted in rage, but he didn't falter. With one final, bone-shattering squeeze, Jada went limp in his arms. Draven tossed her body to the side like a rag doll, his attention now on the others. "Zuri!" Steve shouted as she handed him the mask. His voice cracked with desperation. "The mask gave him power. We have to stop him!" Zuri, Faith, Darnell, Steve, and Naomi formed a circle around Draven. Their faces were set with grim determination.

The flames from the fire raging through the ship flickered and danced in the dark sky. They cast long shadows over the deck as the group braced for the final fight.

Draven, his eyes wild with fury, advanced on them. Despite the mask being removed, his strength hadn't waned. He swung wildly. The group fought with all they had. They dodged, struck, and worked together to bring him down. Every punch, stab, and blow barely slowed him. His rage gave him monstrous power. In the chaos of the fight, Zuri, in a moment of hesitation, slipped on the blood-slicked deck. It was all Draven needed. He grabbed her by the throat, lifting her off the ground with ease. Zuri's eyes widened in fear, and she clawed at his arm, but Draven was beyond reason. With a terrifying growl, he snapped her neck, her body dropping lifelessly to the floor.

"No!" Steve shouted, his voice raw with grief as he watched Zuri fall. The fire roared louder, the ship starting to crack and groan as the flames consumed it.

Smoke billowed around them, making it hard to breathe, but the fight was far from over. Draven, his chest heaving with labored breaths, stood in the center of the inferno. His eyes were bloodshot. His face twisted with madness. His body, though bleeding and bruised, was still a force. The remaining survivors Steve, Faith, Darnell, and Naomi knew this was it. One final push to end the nightmare. "We end this now," Steve muttered, gripping the mask tightly in his hands.

He looked at the others, his face determined, despite the grief weighing on his heart. Draven's reign of terror had to end here, on this burning ship, or none of them would make it out alive. The ship's deck groaned under the weight of destruction. The flames consumed everything in their path. And in the midst of it all, the final battle raged on. As the wail of police sirens pierced the air, Steve's heart pounded. They were close, but the battle wasn't over. Draven, even after everything, refused to fall. His breaths came in ragged gasps, his movements slow but still deadly. The ship groaned, teetering on the brink of ruin. Flames licked the sky as the fire consumed it.

Darnell, his hands trembling, found a bow and arrow amidst the wreckage. His face set with grim determination, he notched an arrow, drew it back, and aimed directly at Draven. With a deep breath, he let the arrow fly.

The arrow whistled through the smoke-filled air, hitting its target with brutal precision. It pierced Draven's eye, a sickening thud echoing as the sharp point embedded itself deep into his skull. Draven stumbled, his hands clawing at his face, blood pouring from the wound. He let out a howl of pain, finally collapsing to the deck, his massive frame hitting the floor with a heavy thud. Steve didn't hesitate. This was their moment, their chance to end Draven's reign of terror for good. He rushed forward, grabbing Draven's limp body and dragging him toward the edge of the ship. The flames were creeping closer, the heat unbearable, but Steve's focus was unshakable. With a final grunt of effort, Steve hoisted Draven over the edge and into the water below.

The splash echoed, and for a moment, it seemed like it was over. But Steve wasn't taking any chances. He still had the mask in his hand, the object that had fueled Draven's power and madness. Steve looked at the burning wreckage of the ship. Its once-majestic frame was now falling apart in the inferno. He picked up a smoldering piece of debris, his hands shaking but resolute. He tied the mask to the chunk of burning wood, ensuring it would sink with Draven and never be found again. With one last look at the water, Steve hurled the wreckage into the sea. He watched as the flames hissed and sizzled on contact. The mask, along with Draven, disappeared into the dark depths of the ocean. The nightmare was over or so they hoped. As the police boats arrived, their lights cut through the smoke. Steve, Darnell, Naomi, and Faith stood on the edge of the burning ship. Their bodies were exhausted and their minds numb. The fire raged on behind them. But, the monster that had terrorized them was no more.

It lay in the water. Ten minutes later, Scarlett saw Draven, floating in the deep. His body was battered, but still intact. Kingston swam to him. He wrapped his arms around Draven's massive form and pulled him toward the surface.

When he finally breached the surface, Scarlett stood on the boat, her face tight with concern. "What happened to him?" she asked as Kingston hoisted Draven's body onto the deck. "He's alive," Kingston said, struggling to catch his breath, "but barely." We need to get him out of here before anyone else shows up." Scarlett glanced at Draven, her gaze lingering on the deep wound where Darnell's arrow had struck. Then her eyes drifted to the water. "Where is his mask?" She asked with a sense of urgency. Kingston froze for a moment, his eyes following Scarlett's to the dark ocean below. "The mask?" He looked around the wreckage, but it was gone, swallowed by the sea along with the flaming debris. "Go get it," Scarlett commanded, her voice icy with determination. Without hesitation, Kingston dived back into the water. He swam deep, the weight of the ocean pressing in on him as he searched for the mask that had fueled Draven's power. Time seemed to stretch. But, finally, his fingers brushed something hard and familiar with the mask. He pulled it from the ocean floor, the weight of it heavy in his hand as he rose to the surface.

Kingston climbed back onto the boat, dripping wet and gasping for air, but victorious. He held up the mask for Scarlett to see. She nodded, satisfied. Without a word, Kingston knelt beside Draven's body and carefully placed the mask back on his face. For a moment, nothing happened. The boat rocked gently in the water, the only sound the distant crackle of flames from the shipwreck. Then, slowly, Draven's body twitched.

Kingston stood up, his eyes wide with anticipation. "Let's go, Scarlett," he said, his voice filled with urgency. "He's waking up." As the boat's engine roared to life and they sped away, Draven stirred. His breaths grew deeper and stronger. Scarlett glanced back at the shipwreck one last time before her gaze returned to Draven. The mask was back where it belonged, and the monster they had revived was far from done.

www.ingramcontent.com/pod-product-compliance
Lightning Source LLC
LaVergne TN
LVHW051034070526
838201LV00009B/193